The
Sherlock Holmes
Crossword Puzzle
Book II

also by Ruth Lake Tepper

The Sherlock Holmes Crossword Puzzle Book

The Sherlock Holmes Crossword Puzzle Book II

Famous Adventures
Fascinating Features
Including
The Hound of the Baskervilles
    (told in 10 puzzles)

by RUTH LAKE TEPPER

With original illustrations by SIDNEY PAGET

W · W · *Norton & Company* · *New York* · *London*

Library of Congress Cataloging in Publication Data
Tepper, Ruth Lake.
    The Sherlock Holmes crossword puzzle book II.
    1. Crossword puzzles.   2. Doyle, Arthur Conan,
Sir, 1859–1930—Characters—Sherlock Holmes.   I. Title.
GV1507.C7T46   793.7'3   79–21036
ISBN 0–0393–00947–5

1 2 3 4 5 6 7 8 9 0

Dear Reader,

How often in our daily lives do we search for solutions to problems—
only to find dusty answers or none at all. So for centuries we have
turned for divertissement to problems that we know can be solved—
puzzles specially created for our wits to unravel. In ancient Greece
they were riddles; in Rome, word games and squares. Today our
favorites are crosswords and detective stories.

In this book I have again combined Sherlock Holmes mysteries with
crossword puzzles. Each story is told in condensed form and includes
the problem, the action, and the clues, but not the solution—that will
be found among the words of the crossword puzzle that accompanies
the story. Solve the puzzle, fill in the spaces below it, and presto—the
solution. On the answer page for each crossword puzzle is an entertain-
ing epilogue to the mystery. (Again, intriguing glimpses of Sherlock
Holmes and his world are featured between puzzles.)

In addition to the short adventures, I have included a complete novel, The
Hound of the Baskervilles, *told in ten abridged, suspenseful parts, each with
its own crossword puzzle and solution. Instead of an epilogue on the answer page,
there is "A Retrospection" after the last puzzle, just as in Conan Doyle's novel.*

So, to old acquaintances and new, happy solving!

Ruth Lake Tepper

Holmes shows Watson a memento from his large tin box of case records.

Contents

STORIES & PUZZLES   9

I.	*The Boscombe Valley Mystery*	10
II.	*The Five Orange Pips*	16
III.	*The Adventure of the Blue Carbuncle*	22
	Did You Know That . . .?	26
	And Did You Know That . . .?	28
IV.	*The Adventure of the Copper Beeches*	30
V.	*The Yellow Face*	36
VI.	*The "Gloria Scott"—Part 1*	40
VII.	*The "Gloria Scott"—Part 2*	44
	The Real Holmes	48
	The Real Watson	49
VIII.	*The Musgrave Ritual*	50
IX.	*The Adventure of the Solitary Cyclist*	56
	Professor Moriarty (Sss!!)	62
X.	*The Adventure of the Priory School—Part 1*	64
XI.	*The Adventure of the Priory School—Part 2*	68
XII.	*The Adventure of the Second Stain*	72
	Intriguing Unpublished Cases	78
	The Gourmets of Baker Street	79

THE HOUND OF THE BASKERVILLES   81

XIII.	*The Curse of the Baskervilles*	82
XIV.	*The Problem*	88
XV.	*Three Broken Threads*	92
XVI.	*The Stapletons of Merripit House*	98

XVII.	*Report of Dr. Watson*	104
XVIII.	*Extract from the Diary of Dr. Watson*	110
XIX.	*The Man on the Tor*	116
XX.	*Death on the Moor*	122
XXI.	*Fixing the Nets*	126
XXII.	*The Hound of the Baskervilles*	132
	A Retrospection	138

SOLUTIONS & EPILOGUES   141

SOLUTIONS TO THE HOUND OF THE BASKERVILLES   155

Stories & Puzzles

The Boscombe Valley Mystery

Hurrying into Paddington Station in response to a wire from Sherlock Holmes, Dr. Watson found his tall, thin friend, dressed in his long travelling cloak, pacing up and down the platform.

"Have you read of the Boscombe Valley tragedy?" asked Holmes, as they boarded the train for Boscombe Valley in Herefordshire.

"Not a word. I have not seen a paper for some days."

They were alone in the carriage, so Holmes could speak freely.

"Inspector Lestrade claims to have a serious case against the murdered man's son. He has sent for me only at the request of a Miss Alice Turner. I will tell you what I have learned so far.

"The largest landed proprietor in Boscombe Valley is Mr. John Turner, who made his money in Australia and returned to England some years ago. One of his farms was let to Mr. Charles McCarthy, also from Australia, where the two had met. While Turner was much the richer man, they were on terms of perfect equality and were often seen together. It was McCarthy who was murdered.

"Turner has an only child, Miss Alice, a lass of eighteen, recently returned from boarding school; McCarthy had only his son James, also eighteen. Both Turner and McCarthy were widowers.

"On June 3rd, Monday last, McCarthy left his farmhouse in the afternoon, and headed for Boscombe Pool, about a quarter-mile distant, telling his serving man that he had an important appointment there. Two people saw him walking alone on his way—an old woman, and Turner's gamekeeper, who also said that minutes after McCarthy passed by, his son James followed—with a gun under his arm.

"Boscombe Pool is a small lake, wooded round, with a fringe of grass about the edge. The young daughter of Turner's lodge keeper was in the woods picking flowers when she saw, close by the lake, McCarthy and his son having a violent quarrel. Frightened, she ran home and told her mother. Just then James came running up to the lodge to say he had found his father dead. He did not have his gun, and his right hand and sleeve were stained with blood.

"The elder McCarthy was found on the grass beside the pool; the left side of the back of his head had been beaten with a blunt weapon, possibly with the butt-end of his son's gun, which lay nearby. James was arrested, the inquest jury returned a verdict of 'wilful murder,' and the case has been referred to the next Assizes."

"What was James's own account at the inquest?" asked Watson.

"He said he had been away at Bristol for three days, returning Monday afternoon. His father was not at home. Looking out of his window, James saw his father return from a drive and walk away from the farm. He was not aware of his father's destination. With his gun, James set out for the warren at

Boscombe Pool. Nearing the pool, he heard a cry of 'Cooee,' the usual signal between his father and himself, and wondered how his father knew he had come home. James admitted the quarrel, but would not state its cause. His father raging, James started for home, but had gone only 150 yards when he heard a hideous cry. He ran back—his father lay dying. He dropped his gun and held him in his arms. The only clear words his father spoke were 'a rat.'

"A point of interest—James said that when he ran back to the lake he saw a gray cloak on the ground a dozen yards from his father. When he left, it was gone—he had had his back to it. I believe James's entire story: he did not try to invent a cause for the quarrel to gain the jury's sympathy, and the words 'a rat' and the vanishing cloak are too *outré* for him to have invented."

Holmes and Watson found Lestrade of Scotland Yard waiting with a carriage to take them to their hotel suite. At tea, Lestrade remarked, "Plain as a pikestaff, young McCarthy is guilty, but one can't refuse Miss Turner. Why, here is her carriage."

A beautiful young woman rushed into the sitting room, her violet eyes shining with excitement and concern.

"Oh, Mr. Holmes," she cried, "I know that James didn't do it, I know it! He is too tenderhearted to hurt a fly!"

"You may rely on my doing all that I can," said Holmes.

"I am sure he refused to speak of the quarrel because I was concerned in it. Mr. McCarthy was anxious that James and I marry, but we loved each other as brother and sister—and James did not wish—"

Her quick blush belied the words about her feelings.

"And was your father in favor of such a union?"

"No, no one but Mr. McCarthy was in favor of it."

"May I see your father if I call tomorrow?"

"The doctor won't allow it. Father has been ill for years, but this has broken him—Mr. McCarthy was the only man alive who had known Dad at the gold mines in Victoria. Oh, please help James!"

When she had gone, Lestrade said that he had permission to take Holmes, but not Watson, to the prison to visit James that night.

Holmes returned late and alone; Lestrade had other lodgings.

"I thought young McCarthy was screening someone, but now I am convinced he is as puzzled as we are about the murder," said Holmes. "He is not very quick-witted, but comely, and sound at heart."

Next morning Holmes was pleased that the weather had continued clear since the day of the crime; the scene would be unmarred. He and Watson joined Lestrade in his cab to visit McCarthy's farm.

"Old Turner is so ill, he may die," reported Lestrade. "He was a friend and benefactor of McCarthy—gave him the farm rent-free."

"Odd," said Holmes, "that McCarthy, who had so little, would quarrel with James for not proposing marriage to a future heiress, as though it were just a case of proposal, and all else would follow."

"The boots her master wore."

At the farm, Holmes asked McCarthy's maid for the boots her master wore at the time of his death, also for a pair of the son's. He measured them, and the three men left for Boscombe Pool.

On the marshy ground round the pool and on the short grass which bounded it were marks of many feet. Holmes examined every mark with his lens, at times lying down on his waterproof.

"Here are your footprints all over the place, Lestrade," said he. "Here's where the party with the lodge keeper came. Here are young McCarthy's feet, twice walking, once running—bearing out his story. Here are his father's feet as he paced up and down. Ah, what's this? Tiptoes! Square, quite unusual boots. They come, go, come again—that was for the cloak! Now where did they come from?"

Watson and Lestrade followed Holmes as he tracked the prints to the woods' edge, where he stopped. Looking round, he picked up a rough stone, put some cigar ash into an envelope, then followed a pathway through the woods to the highroad. Turner's lodge stood nearby. Saying he wanted to have a word with the keeper, Holmes asked Watson and Lestrade to walk on to the cab.

Joining them in moments, Holmes handed the stone to Lestrade.

"This is the murder weapon," he said. "Grass was growing under it; it had lain there only a few days."

"And the murderer?" asked Lestrade.

"Is a tall man, left-handed, limps with the right leg, wears thick-soled shoes and a gray cloak, and smokes Indian cigars."

"I can't go looking for a left-handed man with a game leg," sneered Lestrade. "I'd be the laughingstock of Scotland Yard."

Holmes and Watson returned to their hotel. After lunch, Holmes, who had been pensive, said, "I know who the murderer is. Two points led me to the solution: McCarthy's cry of 'Cooee' before seeing James, and his words 'a rat.' 'Cooee' is an Australian cry; I have to assume McCarthy was awaiting an Australian. As to the 'rat,' I wired to Bristol for this last night."

From his pocket he took a map of the Colony of Victoria, and putting his hand over part of it, he asked, "What do you read?"

"Why, 'ARAT,' " said Watson, astonished.

Holmes raised his hand, and the word "BALLARAT" appeared.

"An Australian from Ballarat," said Holmes, "with a gray cloak. From his footsteps I know that he is tall and lame, and from McCarthy's injuries, that he is left-handed. The culprit is—"

"Mr. John Turner," cried the hotel waiter, opening the door.

A huge old man with limping step and bowed shoulders entered. His hard, craggy face was ashen; he appeared to be deathly ill.

"Pray sit down," said Holmes gently. "You had my note?"

"The lodge keeper brought it," said Turner, sinking his face in his hands. "God help me, but I would have spoken if it went against James at the Assizes. My arrest will break Alice's heart."

"It may not come to that," said Holmes. "Just tell the truth. I shall jot down the facts, you will sign the paper, and Watson will witness it. I will use it only if need be to save James."

"McCarthy blasted my life," began Turner. "In Australia I had got among bad companions, the Ballarat Gang. One day we attacked a gold convoy and killed the escort, but spared the wagon driver, this man McCarthy. We got the gold. I came to England a rich man; I married, and turned a new leaf. I met McCarthy accidentally, and he got his grip on me. My Alice knew nothing of my past. I gave McCarthy everything he wanted to keep him quiet, until he wanted Alice for his son. There I stood firm. McCarthy threatened. We were to meet at the pool to talk it over. When I got there, I overheard him urging his son to marry Alice. It drove me mad. I did it, Mr. Holmes, I'd do it again! McCarthy's cry brought back his son. I had gained the wood, but I was forced to go back for my cloak. That is the true story."

The old man signed the paper and tottered from the room.

"He shall soon answer for his deeds at a higher court than the Assizes," observed Holmes. "Young James will be free."

"Why was James so averse to marrying Alice?" wondered Watson.

"He told me of his plight," said Holmes. "He's madly in love with her now, but he had had a very good reason not to propose."

What was James's reason for not proposing? Did you guess?

13

Across

1 Herring's kin
5 Phooey!
8 Empire State flower
12 ". . . ___-cake, baker's man"
13 Khayyám
15 Sra. Perón
17 Word before smasher or bomb
18 Military assistant
19 ___ one with (saw eye to eye)
20 Put in shape
22 Pound-___
24 Companion of whiskey
26 Lizard: Comb. form
27 Softy
31 Nosy Parkers
35 Prince Henry, to Falstaff
36 All over
38 Connecting peg
39 "It's pretty, but ___ Art?"
41 Dead duck

43 "I never ___ man I didn't like"
44 Lesson, at the lycée
46 Subleased
48 Minded the baby
49 Varnish resins
51 Sub rosa
53 The shivers
55 Stock-exchange membership
56 What one good turn deserves
59 Group of fish
63 Robinson Crusoe's creator
64 Proverbs
67 Sea eagle
68 River in Virginia
69 General Robert ___
70 Pied Piper's prey
71 Nuisance
72 Commercials
73 Kind of machine

Down

1 Jib boom, for example
2 Abominate
3 Sleep like ___
4 Napery fabric
5 Light timber
6 ". . . ___ my brother's keeper?"
7 ___ on (wore)
8 Reversed, as tape
9 White House office
10 Alfonso's agreement
11 Greek letters
14 Relatives of umps
16 Disbeliever in God: Abbr.
21 Hercules's captive
23 Western Hemisphere assoc.
25 Phrase of option
27 Period of time
28 Gauguin's gear
29 Wonderland's child
30 They transmit hereditary characteristics

32 "Lend less than thou ___"
33 Part of a corolla
34 Bluish gray
37 Printers' marks
40 Love apples
42 Niches
45 Closest
47 Tric___ (backgammon)
50 Litigate
52 Anesthetics
54 Gaelic
56 Part of speech: Abbr.
57 Kind of tide
58 "Speak ___ as I am . . ."
60 Homonym of aural
61 Aware of: Slang
62 For fear that
65 ___ mode
66 Weekday, for short

Puzzle I: *The Boscombe Valley Mystery*

Solution and epilogue on page 142

| 22 Across | 68 Across | 7 Down | 51 Across |

| 66 Down | 56 Across | 27 Down | 29 Down |

| 19 Across | 5 Down | 59 Across |

15

The Five Orange Pips

A howling gale beat against the windows of 221B Baker Street one dark night of September of 1887, but inside the snug sitting room Sherlock Holmes was at work on his records, and Dr. Watson, who was staying with Holmes while Mrs. Watson was away on a visit, was deep in a sea story. Suddenly, the bell rang.

"If it's a client," said Holmes, "the case is most serious."

The man who entered following the ring was about twenty-two, well-groomed, trimly clad, with refinement in his bearing.

"I owe you an apology," he said. He appeared to be weighted down with a great anxiety. "I have come for advice and help."

"Please sit down," said Holmes, indicating a chair near the fire, "and favor me with some details of your trouble."

"I am John Openshaw," said the young man, "but my affairs have little to do with the awful business. It is a hereditary matter.

"My grandfather had two sons—my uncle Elias and my father Joseph, who was a successful manufacturer in Coventry. My uncle Elias had emigrated to America as a young man; there he became a rich planter in Florida. He was a colonel in the Confederate Army, and when the Civil War was over he returned to his plantation. About 1869 he came back to England and took a small estate near Horsham. His reason for leaving the States was his aversion to black people; he did not want them to vote.

"My uncle was a fierce, solitary man. He never set foot outside his estate; he took his exercise in the garden round his house.

"When my father and I visited him in 1878, my uncle begged my father to let me live with him. My father agreed, and by the time I was sixteen I was quite master of the house. I kept the keys and could go where I liked, with one exception—my uncle had an attic room, always locked; no one was permitted to enter.

"One day—it was in March 1883—a letter from India came for my uncle. 'Pondicherry postmark!' he cried. 'What can this be?' He opened it, and out there fell upon the table five dried orange pips. 'K. K. K.!' he shrieked, pale and trembling.

" 'What is it, uncle?' I cried.

" 'Death,' said he. I took up the envelope; there was no letter in it, only three K's marked in red ink on the inner flap.

" 'Send for my lawyer,' instructed my uncle.

"When the lawyer arrived, I took him to my uncle's bedroom. A fire was burning brightly, and in the grate was a mass of ashes, as of burned paper, while a brass box stood open and empty beside it. I saw, with a start, that the lid was printed with the treble K.

" 'I wish you, John,' said my uncle, 'to witness my will. I leave my estate to your father, whose heir you no doubt will be.'

"Weeks passed; my uncle began to drink heavily. He would emerge from his room in a frenzy and tear about the garden with a revolver. One night he made a drunken sally from which he never came back. We found him face downward in a little pool in the garden. As there was no sign of violence, the jury, knowing of my uncle's eccentricities, brought in a verdict of 'suicide.'"

"One moment," said Holmes. "Let me have the date your uncle received the envelope, and the date of his supposed suicide."

"The envelope arrived March 10th, and my uncle died May 2nd, seven weeks later. My father and I found the brass K. K. K. box in the attic room. Inside the lid of the empty box was a paper label reading 'Letters, memoranda, and a register.'

"In 1884 my father came to live at Horsham. On January 4, 1885, another blow fell. We were at breakfast, when my father opened an envelope and out fell five orange pips.

" 'It is the K. K. K.!' I exclaimed.

" 'Yes,' he said. 'Here are the K's. Above them is written, "Put the papers on the sundial." What papers? What sundial?'

" 'The sundial in the garden; there is no other,' said I. 'But the papers must be those that were burned.'

" 'Pooh,' said my father. 'Where does this tomfoolery come from?'

" 'From Dundee,' I answered, glancing at the postmark.

"I wanted to notify the police, but he forbade it. Less than a week after receiving the envelope, my father was dead. He had gone to visit a friend near Portdown Hill and had been killed falling into one of the deep chalk pits which abound there. As the pit was unfenced, the jury's verdict was 'death from accidental causes.' In this sinister way, I came into my inheritance. Now, the blow has fallen on me."

Openshaw took from his waistcoat a crumpled envelope, and turning to the table he shook out upon it five dried orange pips.

"The postmark is London—eastern division," he said. "Within are the same words: 'K. K. K.' and 'Put the papers on the sundial.'"

"What have you done?" asked Holmes.

"Nothing. I have felt helpless. I have seen the police, but they smiled at my story. However, they have allowed me a policeman, to remain in my house."

"Incredible imbecility! Why did he not come with you tonight?" cried Holmes. "Now, have you no further detail which may help?"

Openshaw put a piece of blue-tinted paper on the table. "I found this sheet on the floor of my uncle's room. The unburned margins of the burned papers were of this particular color. The writing is undoubtedly my uncle's."

Holmes and Watson bent over the paper; it was headed "March, 1869," and beneath were the following notices:

> 7 th. *Set pips on McCauley, Paramore, and John Swain.*
> 10 th. *McCauley and John Swain cleared.*
> 12 th. *Visited Paramore. All well.*

" 'All well' was death for Paramore; you must act at once," said Holmes. "Put this paper into the brass box, with a note swearing that all other papers were burned. Put the box upon the sundial. We must first remove the danger which threatens you, and then find and punish the guilty parties. How do you go back?"

"By train from Waterloo."

"It is not yet nine; the crowded streets will protect you."

"I am armed," said Openshaw. "Shall I see you at Horsham?"

"No, your secret lies in London; I shall seek it here."

After Openshaw left, Holmes sat silent for some time.

"The nature of the peril is clear," he said at length.

"Who is this K. K. K.?" cried Watson.

"Kindly hand me down the letter K of the American Encyclopedia. Thank you. Colonel Openshaw's leaving of America and his solitude in England suggest that he was in fear of someone or something. Did you remark the postmarks of those letters?"

"Pondicherry, Dundee, and London," said Watson.

"East London. What do you deduce from that?"

"They are all seaports. The writers were on board ship."

"Excellent," said Holmes. "In the case of Pondicherry, seven weeks elapsed between the threat and the fulfillment; in Dundee it was less than a week. We must presume that the vessel the men were on is a sailing ship, and that they always sent their letter by steamer before starting on their mission. But the last one is from London—we can't count on delay! Now, for K. K. K."

Holmes opened the encyclopedia and read from it:

> *Ku Klux Klan. This terrible secret society was formed by some ex-Confederate soldiers in the Southern states after the Civil War. Its power was used to terrorize black voters and to murder or drive from the country those who were opposed to its views. Its outrages were usually preceded by a warning to the marked man: melon seeds or orange pips. In 1869 the movement suddenly collapsed, although there have been sporadic outbreaks since that date.*

"When the society collapsed," said Holmes, "Colonel Openshaw fled from America with its papers. The register may implicate some prominent Southerners—who are desperate to recover it."

Next morning the weather had cleared. When Watson came down to breakfast, he found Holmes having coffee before departing for the City to work on Openshaw's case. Picking up the unopened newspaper from the table, Watson suddenly cried, "Holmes! You are too late! Here is the account." He read aloud from the newspaper:

> *Between nine and ten last night, Police-Constable Cook, on duty near Waterloo Bridge, heard a cry for help and a splash in the water. Because of the dark and the storm, it was impossible to effect a rescue, but the body was recovered. It was that of young John Openshaw of Horsham. It is conjectured*

18

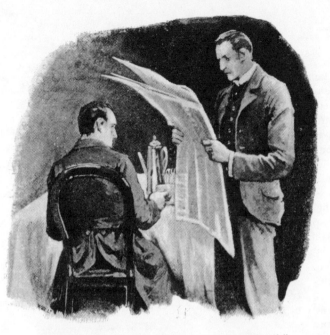

"Watson suddenly cried, 'Holmes! You are too late!'"

that in the darkness he missed his path and walked over the edge of a boat landing. The body exhibited no traces of violence. There can be no doubt that the deceased was the victim of an unfortunate accident.

Holmes was more shaken than Watson had ever seen him.

"That he should have come to me for help, and that I should send him to his death—!" He sprang from his chair and paced about the room in uncontrollable agitation. "Well, Watson, we shall see who will win in the long run. I am going out now!"

It was late in the evening before Holmes returned to Baker Street. He was tired and hungry, but appeared to be triumphant.

"I have them in the hollow of my hand, Watson! Openshaw shall not remain unavenged. Let us put their own trademark on them."

Holmes took an orange from the cupboard, squeezed five pips out on the table, and thrust them into an envelope. On the inside flap he wrote "S. H. for J. O." Then he sealed it and addressed it to "Captain James Calhoun, Bark *Lone Star*, Savannah, Georgia."

"Who is Captain Calhoun? How did you trace him?" asked Watson.

"He is the leader of the gang. I spent the whole day over Lloyd's register and files of old papers, following the future career of every vessel which touched at Pondicherry in January and February in '83. Thirty-six ships reported there during those months. One, the *Lone Star*, instantly attracted my attention."

Why did the bark Lone Star *attract Holmes's attention?*

19

Across

1 ___ Benedict
5 "Watchman, what ___ night?"
10 Hornet
14 Disastrous defeat
15 Combine again
16 Ending for allow or avoid
17 Site of the Taj Mahal
18 Music ___ (Wagnerian opera)
19 Sirius is one
20 ___ lights (aurora australis)
22 Pater's partner
24 Unearthly
25 In the chips
26 Social movements
29 Disputes
33 Land ___ (sleep)
34 They may be magnetic
35 Siamese
36 Ingenuous
37 Subsided
38 Copper
39 School subj.
40 Make one's ___ boil
41 Coat with metal
42 Conscious
44 Whirled
45 Indy 500, for example
46 Isinglass
47 Protoplasm unit: Comb. form
49 Cognomen
53 Walked on
54 ". . . a majority ___"
56 Eye or star
57 Whet
58 "On a tree by a ___ . . ."
59 Flimflam
60 Water pitcher
61 Scorches
62 Very, in Versailles

Down

1 Babylonian, Greek, etc.
2 Energetic: Slang
3 Swami
4 ___ mind (moods)
5 Brotherhoods
6 Charon's boat
7 Fed
8 ". . . let ___ now speak"
9 Investigated
10 "It ___ best of times . . ."
11 Pay to the pot
12 Cliff
13 According to
21 Pay attention
23 Parts of a play
25 Lassoed
26 Ice-cream shells
27 ___ in the Crowd
28 Card or jack
29 Discoverer of North American coast
30 Purloin
31 French aunt
32 Placed on location
34 Kind of steak
37 Qualified voters
38 Least soiled
40 Partiality
41 "A ___ of pickled peppers . . ."
43 Merchant
44 Kitchen utensils
46 Gold digger
47 Ship's bow
48 ___ wolf
49 Variable star
50 Assert
51 1,760 yards
52 Pipe joints
53 Comb. form meaning "a god"
55 For shame!

Puzzle II: *The Five Orange Pips*

1	2	3	4		5	6	7	8	9		10	11	12	13
14					15						16			
17					18						19			
20			21					22	23					
		24					25							
26	27	28				29					30	31	32	
33				34					35					
36			37					38						
39		40					41							
42		43				44								
	45			46										
47	48			49				50	51	52				
53			54	55			56							
57			58				59							
60			61				62							

Solution and epilogue on page 143

___ ___ ___ ___ ___ ___ ___ ___ ___ ___

48 Down   19 Across   10 Down   49 Across

___ ___ ___ ___ ___ ___ ___ ___ ___ ___ ___ ___

54 Across   5 Across   20 Across

___ ___ ___ ___ ___ ___ ___ ___ ___ ___ ___ ___ ___ ___ .

4 Down   53 Down   28 Down

The Adventure of the Blue Carbuncle

The second morning after Christmas, Dr. Watson, calling on his friend Sherlock Holmes, found him studying a disreputable hat of black hard-felt, which hung at an angle on a chair.

"This trophy belongs to Peterson, the commissionaire," said Holmes. "He found it. On Christmas morning he was on his way home when he saw a man, carrying a goose, being attacked by a knot of roughs. They had knocked the man's hat off, and he, raising his stick to defend himself, smashed the shop window behind him. Peterson ran to help, but frightened by his uniform, the man dropped the goose and fled, as did the roughs, leaving Peterson with the spoils. He brought them to me. Peterson has the goose. The bird was addressed to 'Mrs. Henry Baker,' and the hat is initialled 'H. B.,' but there are hundreds of Henry—"

Just then the door flew open and Peterson rushed in.

"See what my wife found in the goose's crop!" he gasped, displaying a brilliantly scintillating blue stone.

"The Countess of Morcar's carbuncle!" cried Holmes. "A reward of £1000, Peterson—it's been advertised in *The Times* lately! I have the newspaper account—here it is." He read aloud:

> *Hotel Cosmopolitan Jewel Robbery. John Horner, 26, was charged with stealing the Countess of Morcar's precious blue carbuncle. James Ryder, head attendant at the hotel, said he had shown Horner up to the Countess's dressing room on the 22d. inst., to solder the grate. Ryder had been called away; on returning to the room he found that Horner had disappeared, the bureau had been forced open, and the jewel case lay empty. He gave the alarm, and Horner was arrested, struggling and protesting his innocence. The stone could not be found. Catherine Cusack, maid to the Countess, corroborated Ryder's evidence. Horner has a previous conviction for robbery.*

"The evidence against Horner is circumstantial. We must ascertain Baker's part in this mystery," said Holmes, writing out an advertisement asking Baker to apply to 221B Baker Street for hat and goose. "Have the agency put this in all the evening papers, Peterson, and buy me a goose. Thank you. I'll keep the stone. Come round tonight, Watson; it may prove interesting."

That evening Watson and Baker, whose rusty black coat matched his hat, arrived at the same time. Baker's alarm at finding his goose gone vanished when Holmes presented him with a substitute.

"I wonder where you got *your* goose—a rare one," said Holmes.

"Mr. Windigate of the Alpha Inn started a goose club; we paid our pence weekly to get a bird at Christmas," explained Baker.

On Baker's departure, Holmes suggested to Watson that a trip to the Alpha Inn be made at once. Mr. Windigate proved to be a genial, obliging man who told them he had purchased two dozen geese for his club from a Mr. Breckenridge at Covent Garden.

Breckenridge was not so obliging. When Holmes asked him where he had bought the birds that he had sold to Mr. Windigate, Breckenridge burst out angrily, "One would think they're the only geese in the world, for all the questions about them!"

Holmes wagered a fiver that the birds were country bred. Breckenridge declared him a loser and took out his ledger to prove it. "See here. 'Bought from Mrs. Oakshott, 117 Brixton Road, December 22d, 24 geese at 7s. 6d.' And underneath, 'Sold to Mr. Windigate of the Alpha, at 12s.'"

Holmes paid the useful wager, and he and Watson had walked on some few yards, when a loud hubbub broke out from the stall they had just left. Breckenridge was shaking his fist fiercely at a little, rat-faced man, and shouting, "I've had enough of you and your geese! Did I buy the geese off you?"

"Mrs. Oakshott can tell you one of them was mine."

"Get out of here!" shouted Breckenridge.

As the man moved away, Holmes whispered to Watson, "Ha! This may save us a visit to Brixton Road." He overtook the little man and touched him on the shoulder. The man sprang round.

"Who are you? What do you want?" he quavered.

"I think I can be of assistance to you," said Holmes.

"Who are you? What could you know of the matter?"

"My name is Sherlock Holmes. I know you are trying to trace some geese that were sold by Mrs. Oakshott to Mr. Breckenridge, who sold them to Mr. Windigate, who sold them to his club."

"Oh, sir, you're the very one I have wanted to meet," cried the man. "I cannot tell you how interested I am in the matter!"

"Now, sir, I should like to know your name," said Holmes.

The man hesitated. "My name is John Robinson," he said.

Holmes hailed a four-wheeler, and he and Watson and their guest set off for Baker Street.

"Here we are!" said Holmes, as they entered the warm sitting room. "Pray take a chair. Now, you want to know what became of the geese, or rather, I fancy, of that goose. It was one bird you were interested in—white, with a black-barred tail."

"Oh, sir, can you tell me where it went to?"

"It came here. And it laid the bonniest blue egg that was ever seen. I have it here in my museum."

Holmes unlocked his strongbox and held up the carbuncle.

The little man glared, uncertain whether to claim or disown it.

"The game is up, sir," said Holmes. " 'John Robinson' is an alias. I know your real name, and I know you stole this jewel."

The man's claim to one of the geese, and his alias, in itself, were clues to Holmes. Did you guess who 'John Robinson' was?

Across

1 Exclamations of contempt
5 Lackaday!
9 "_____ Johnny!"
14 Kind of jacket
15 German refusal
16 Give the slip
17 Concomitant
19 Carl Maria von _____
20 In _____ (ahead)
21 Credentials
22 School cheers
23 Rough
25 Currents
28 Not _____ (to no degree)
32 Butter unit
35 Game-bird ragout
36 "This little pig had _____ "
37 Auricular
39 Stewart or Cagney

41 Joyce Carol Oates novel
42 Island of the armless Venus
43 To have, in Havana
45 Snooze
46 " _____ , Brute!"
47 Athletes' shirts
49 Requirements
51 Room-furnishing scheme
55 Attacked
58 "At _____ the time will be . . ."
60 Climbing plants
61 Different from
63 Word in an Austen title
64 Seed covering
65 Disembark
66 Fourth estate
67 South African monetary unit
68 Partner of odds

Down

1 Like bog fuel
2 _____ drop of a hat
3 Motel's progenitor
4 Fishhook lines
5 ". . . for a year _____ day"
6 Beer top
7 Sixty sec.
8 Ending for cad or par
9 " _____ not of an age . . ."
10 P. T. Barnum's *Jumbo*
11 Hayseed
12 River in Germany
13 Preachments: Abbr.
18 Cozy places
21 Kings' sons, for short
23 Sledges
24 City on the Somme
26 Sovereignty, in India
27 Jubilant
29 Fourth book of the New Testament
30 "_____ penny, two a penny . . ."

31 Impermanent, for short
32 Apple, for example
33 In harness
34 Joust
38 Wife of an earl
40 Bishopric
44 U. S. painter Albert Pinkham
47 Squirt
48 Colonize
50 Facilitates
52 George M.
53 _____ on (continuously)
54 Tears apart
55 "A _____ of fog betwixt . . ."
56 Incessantly
57 Number of Muses
58 Lacking substance
59 Clutched
61 Put one's _____ in (meddle)
62 Musical syllable

Puzzle III:
The Adventure of the Blue Carbuncle

Solution and epilogue on page 144

___ ___ ___ ___ ___ ___ ___ ___ ___ ___

9 Down 36 Across 61 Across

___ ___ ___ ___ ___ ___ ___ , ___ ___ ___ ___ ___ ___ ___

39 Across 44 Down 6 Down 17 Across

___ ___ ___ ___ ___ ___ ___ , ___ ___ ___ ___ .

2 Down 38 Down 3 Down

Did You Know That . . . ?

● Conan Doyle became deeply involved in spiritualism in his later life, devoting most of his time and energy to promoting its cause in books and lectures. He was a strong champion of mediums and a believer in séances. In his book, *The Case for Spirit Photography*, he defended a photographer accused of fraud. The prolific photographer, who also held séances and went into trances, had produced pictures showing live persons with the spirit of a beloved departed relative, made corporeal, hovering nearby. Many such pictures illustrate Doyle's book.

● The war wound suffered by Dr. Watson at the battle of Maiwand in Afghanistan was one of the causes of his being returned to England and thus of his historic meeting with Sherlock Holmes. In *A Study in Scarlet* the wound is described as a shattered bone in his shoulder. But in *The Sign of Four* the wound has moved to his leg, all the way down to his Achilles tendon.

● In their book, *Theory of Games and Economic Behavior*, the great physicist and mathematician, Dr. John von Neumann, and the famous economic theorist, Professor Oskar Morgenstern, demonstrated mathematically that Conan Doyle, in "The Final Problem," had intuitively chosen the right route for Holmes to take to elude Professor Moriarty when Holmes fled from London to the Continent. (This, of course, did not prevent the evil professor from eventually tracking Holmes to Switzerland and catching up with him at the Reichenbach Falls.)

● Although Sherlock Holmes is most frequently pictured smoking a calabash pipe, he was a prodigious smoker of all forms of tobacco. Smoking helped him to think. When Inspector Bradstreet, in "The Man with the Twisted Lip," said wistfully, "I wish I knew how you reach your results," Holmes told him, ". . . by sitting upon five pillows and consuming an ounce of shag." Holmes owned a variety of pipes, including a black clay, a brierroot, and a long cherry-wood. His usual pipe smoke was a strong, coarse shag. His cigar case was always filled and was generously available to addicted acquaintances. He used his silver cigarette case as a paperweight to hold down his farewell note to Watson at the Reichenbach Falls. An expert on tobacco ashes, Holmes wrote a monograph on the subject; in it he enumerated a hundred and forty forms of cigar, cigarette, and pipe tobacco, with colored plates illustrating the differences in the types of ash.

Holmes, with cigar, reviews a case with Watson.

And Did You Know That . . . ?

• Although Sherlock Holmes was a man who seldom took exercise for exercise's sake, he was an expert boxer, having taken up the sport at college. Watson called him "undoubtedly one of the finest boxers of his weight" that he had ever seen; he credited Holmes's good physical condition to his usually spare diet (though Holmes liked fine food, he ate in moderation) and to his generally simple habits. Holmes's fine boxing skills were usually reserved for his encounters with aggressive villains, but once he boxed three rounds with a professional prizefighter on the occasion of a benefit for the fighter. Said that gentleman to Holmes, "Ah, you're one that has wasted your gifts, you have!"

• Among Holmes's other physical skills, he had remarkable powers, carefully cultivated, of seeing in the dark.

• Conan Doyle's active and imaginative mind and his extraordinary versatility often led him to fields far removed from writing. At the beginning of World War I, he started to study ways and means of protecting Britain's fighting men. Largely due to his efforts, troops embarking for France were equipped with inflatable rubber collars and their ships carried inflatable lifeboats. Doyle was the first to advocate metal helmets, and the British tin hat was introduced in 1916. (In 1902 Doyle had been knighted for his work with a field hospital in South Africa during the Boer War, and for his history of the war.)

• At the legendary first meeting of Holmes and Watson, while they were discussing their respective "shortcomings" before renting the Baker Street lodgings, Watson admitted, "I keep a bull pup." But Holmes must have banished the pup in an offstage edict, for he is never heard of again.

• In "The Boscombe Valley Mystery," Inspector Lestrade of Scotland Yard was "retained" by Alice Turner and other friends of James McCarthy to help establish his innocence. (Lestrade, instead, found a good case against young James, whereupon Sherlock Holmes was enlisted in the cause by Miss Turner.) The retaining of official police personnel by individuals or private companies was permitted by the Metropolitan Police Act of 1839.

• As a doctor, Watson was of considerable help to Holmes in some of his cases, but his most noteworthy service to Holmes as a friend and a doctor was to warn him of the dangers of using morphine and cocaine. Holmes had turned to drugs to relieve the terrible boredom that plagued him between cases; it was through Watson's remonstrances that he was gradually weaned from his addiction.

Holmes delivers a straight left to a slogging scoundrel.

The Adventure of the Copper Beeches

The days of the great cases appear to be past," complained Sherlock Holmes to Dr. Watson one morning in spring. "This note marks my zero point. 'I am anxious to consult you as to whether I should accept a certain situation as governess. I shall call at half-past ten. Violet Hunter.' Well, there is her ring."

In a few moments the sitting-room door opened, and in came a neat, brisk, bright-faced young woman, with shining chestnut hair.

"I hope you will excuse my troubling you, Mr. Holmes," she said. "I have no parents or relations to turn to for advice."

"Pray take a seat," said Holmes. "I shall be happy to help."

"I was a governess for five years," said Miss Hunter, "until the family left England two months ago. I applied to an agency for governesses, managed by Miss Stoper. Last week I was shown into Miss Stoper's office and found a very stout man sitting at her elbow. Seeing me, he jumped up and said, 'Capital!' and at once offered me £100 a year—it was too good to be true.

" 'May I ask where you live, and about my duties?' I inquired.

" 'Charming rural place. The Copper Beeches, five miles from Winchester—lovely country house, with a six-year-old boy. My wife and I are rather faddy people, though; she would wish you to cut your hair short. You would not object to her whim?'

" 'I really could not cut my hair,' I replied firmly.

" 'It is a pity,' said he. 'That quite settles the matter.'

"The last few days, I began to regret my decision—I am nearly destitute, Mr. Holmes. Yesterday I had made up my mind to speak to Miss Stoper, when I received this letter from the gentleman himself, Mr. Jephro Rucastle. I shall read it to you:

> *We are willing to pay £120 a year. Our fads are not exacting. My wife would ask you to wear an electric-blue dress indoors in the morning. You need not buy such a dress; we have one belonging to my daughter Alice (now in Philadelphia), which should fit you. As regards your hair, I must remain firm. Do try to come; let me know your train.*

"Before I take the final step, may I ask your advice?"

"Have you formed some opinion of this household?" asked Holmes.

"Mr. Rucastle looked a kind man; perhaps his wife is mad."

"Perhaps. But it doesn't seem a nice place for a young lady."

"But the money, Mr. Holmes! I thought if you knew of the matter, you would understand afterwards if I needed your help."

"If you find yourself in any doubt or danger, a telegram, day or night, would bring me down to help you," said Holmes.

"That is enough." With a few grateful words, she was gone.

"I fear we shall hear from her soon," said Holmes.

Two weeks later Miss Hunter wired, urgently requesting Holmes to come to the Black Swan Hotel in Winchester at noon the following day. Holmes, good as his word, arrived, bringing Watson.

"Pray tell us what has happened to you," said Holmes.

"I have met with no actual ill-treatment from Mr. and Mrs. Rucastle, but I am not easy in my mind about them.

"The Copper Beeches is an old, unlovely square house, with some wooded grounds round it on three sides; in the front a field slopes down a hundred yards to the highroad.

"Mrs. Rucastle is not mad. She is a silent, pale-faced woman of thirty, about fifteen years younger than her husband. He was a widower when they married seven years ago; Alice, the daughter who has gone to Philadelphia, was his only child by the first wife. The most unpleasant thing about the household are the servants, Toller and his wife. He is an uncouth man who drinks; his wife is a tall, strong woman, as silent as Mrs. Rucastle.

"I was at the house three days, when Mr. Rucastle thanked me for cutting my hair and asked me to put on the blue dress and come down to the drawing room. The room stretches along the front of the house and has three long windows. A chair had been placed near the central window, with its back to it, and in this I was asked to sit. Then Mr. Rucastle began to tell me funny stories, and I laughed until I was weary. After an hour or so of this, I was asked to leave and look after the boy.

"Two days later the same performance took place, again with my back to the window. I became curious to know what was going on behind my back. My hand mirror had been broken, and on the next occasion, I hid a piece of the glass in my handkerchief. Then, in the midst of my laughter, I put the handkerchief up to my eyes, and was able to see behind me. There was a small man standing in the highroad, leaning against the railing, and looking up at the window. Mrs. Rucastle noticed what I had done.

" 'Jephro,' said she, 'there is an impertinent fellow on the road staring up at Miss Hunter.'

" 'Turn round, Miss Hunter; wave him away,' said Mr. Rucastle.

"I did as I was told, and Mrs. Rucastle drew the blind. That was a week ago, and I have not sat again in the window."

"Your tale is most interesting," said Holmes. "Pray go on."

"You will find it rather disconnected," said Miss Hunter. "The first day I arrived, Mr. Rucastle took me to a small outhouse and showed me his huge mastiff, which is kept chained in the day and loosed at night. Toller has charge of him. 'It's worth your life if you go out at night,' Mr. Rucastle warned me.

"When I had had my hair cut, I had placed the coil of cut hair in the bottom of my trunk. Last week I pried open a locked drawer in the bureau in my room, for I needed the space, and there was my coil of hair. How *could* it be? I opened my trunk with trembling hands, and there was my own hair. The two coils were identical. I was afraid to say anything to the Rucastles.

"I am naturally observant and had noticed that one side of the house's upper floor was not inhabited; the door to it was locked. One day I saw Mr. Rucastle coming out through this door, an angry look on his face. Going out to that side of the house, I looked up at the windows; two were dirty, the third shuttered.

" 'You have discovered my darkroom,' said Mr. Rucastle, coming up suddenly behind me. 'Photography's my hobby.' He smiled but his eyes were cold. I had chanced on something mysterious.

"Toller and his wife also visit these deserted rooms. Yesterday, Toller, being drunk, left the key in the door, and the coast being clear, I slipped through. In the passage were three doors, two opening into empty rooms, the third locked. Light glimmered from beneath the locked door, and suddenly I heard footsteps within the room. I became terrified, and rushed from the passage, straight into the arms of Mr. Rucastle.

" 'If you ever put foot in there again,' he cried angrily, 'I'll throw you to the mastiff!'

"I ran to my room, trembling. I might have fled the house, but I thought if I could only bring you down all would be well. I have to be back before three o'clock, for Mr. and Mrs. Rucastle will be away all evening, and I must look after the child. Oh, Mr. Holmes, what should I do?"

Holmes had heard Miss Hunter's story with profound gravity.

"Is Toller still drunk?"

"Yes, he's been drunk these last two days."

"That is well. And the Rucastles go out tonight. That leaves Mrs. Toller. Is there a cellar with a strong lock? Good. You are a brave girl, Miss Hunter, and I shall ask you to send Mrs. Toller to the cellar on an errand, and then turn the key on her. By seven o'clock we shall be at the Copper Beeches. It is clear that you were chosen to impersonate Rucastle's daughter Alice, and to convince the man on the highroad—possibly her fiancé—that she is quite happy without him. The dog is loosed at night to prevent him from communicating with her. I have no doubt that she is the prisoner in the locked room. We must help her."

A smiling Miss Hunter awaited Holmes and Watson on the doorstep at seven. They could hear Mrs. Toller pounding on the cellar door. Giving Holmes the keys she had taken from the drunken, sleeping Toller, Miss Hunter led Holmes and Watson upstairs to the third, locked door. Holmes tried the keys, but none fit. No sound came from the room. At Holmes's suggestion, both men put their shoulders to the rickety door; it gave at once. They rushed into the room—the skylight above was open, the prisoner gone.

"Rucastle has carried his victim off through the skylight!" exclaimed Holmes. He swung himself up to look out at the roof. "Yes, here is the end of a ladder."

Suddenly, a very fat man walked in. Miss Hunter screamed.

"You villain!" cried Holmes. "Where is your daughter!"

Rucastle cast his eyes round, and then at the open skylight.

"It is for me to ask you that!" he shrieked. "I'll serve you thieves!" He turned and clattered down the stairs.

"He's gone for the dog!" cried Miss Hunter. As Holmes, followed by Watson and Miss Hunter, rushed down to close the front door, they heard the baying of a hound, and then a scream of agony.

Toller, awakened by the commotion, had staggered in. "My God!" he cried. "The dog has not been fed for two days."

Running outside, Holmes and Watson found the beast at Rucastle's throat. Watson blew its brains out with his revolver, and they carried Rucastle, still alive, into the house. They had all assembled round him, when Mrs. Toller walked in.

"Mr. Rucastle let me out when he came back. Ah, Miss Hunter, I could have told you that your plan was not necessary."

"Ha!" said Holmes. "You know more than we do."

"Yes. It became real bad for Miss Alice when she met Mr. Fowler. She had rights of her own by will, but she had left everything in Mr. Rucastle's hands. He wanted her to sign a paper so he could use her money even if she married. When she refused, he worried her until she got brain fever, and her hair had to be cut off. But Mr. Fowler stuck by her as true as man could be."

"Ah," said Holmes, "I think I can deduce the rest."

Can you? How did Fowler manage to free Alice and escape with her?

"Watson blew its brains out."

Across

1 Title for Dalloway or Quickly
4 Unclouded
9 "____ in disgrace with fortune . . ."
13 Is under the weather
15 Appaloosa, for one
16 ____ done (stop)
17 "The wolf ____ the door!"
18 Brainstorms
19 Tell ____ (deceive)
20 Corrupt
22 Church-bell ringer
24 Individuals
25 Patient
26 Greased the palm of
29 Garrison
30 Titles for Livingstone and Schweitzer
33 Correct, as a clock
34 Speechify
35 Van Winkle
36 Corn spikes
37 Ringlet
38 Melody
39 Thirst quencher
40 Strip of boneless fish
41 Under a strain
42 Elizabethan dramatist
43 Biblical prophet
44 Interlocked
45 Architect who rebuilt St. Paul's
46 Castilian cat
47 ". . . a time ____ , and a time to cast away"
50 Viands
54 ____ out (supplements)
55 Curved
58 Duck or excuse
59 "____ it the truth?"
60 Drench
61 Blue-pencil
62 New York nine
63 Hauler
64 Overhead railways

Down

1 Marian was one
2 Ascent
3 Smelting dross
4 Admonished
5 Bonanzas
6 "Able was I ____ I saw Elba"
7 Sound ____ whistle
8 Makes a new beginning
9 Sulfur-bottom, for example
10 Auditorium
11 Feminine nickname
12 ____ -do-well
14 Disco lights
21 Caught in ____ (entangled)
23 Bone: Comb. form
25 Kind of guard
26 Fracture
27 Willing
28 ". . . fair weather: for the sky ____ "
29 Disengages
30 Under the influence
31 Flush
32 Trap or demon
34 Synthetic fabric
37 "Time present and ____ "
38 Defensible
40 Taxi passenger
41 Small monkey
44 Jacob's ____
45 Actress Mae and writer Rebecca
46 Sillies
47 Crew
48 Migratory worker
49 English county
51 Take on cargo
52 Actor Jannings
53 Coteries
56 Marsupial, in Melbourne
57 Incise

Puzzle IV:
The Adventure of the Copper Beeches

Solution and epilogue on page 145

———— ———— ———— ————. ———— ———— ———— ———— —— ————

26 Across   1 Across   22 Across   47 Across

———— ———— ———— ———————, ———— ———— ————.———— ————

22 Across   30 Down   16 Across   44 Down

———— ———— ———— ———— ———— ———— ————.————.

27 Down   9 Across   25 Down   4 Across

The Yellow Face

M r. Grant Munro, the man disclosing his problem to Sherlock Holmes and Dr. Watson in their sitting room one spring evening, was tall, well dressed, about thirty, and very upset.

"I have been married three years," he was saying. "My wife and I have loved each other truly. But last Monday, a barrier sprang up between us; there is some mystery in her life. But Effie loves me dearly. I know it. I feel it."

"Kindly let me have the facts," said Holmes.

"I'll tell you about Effie. Some years ago she had gone to live in America, in Atlanta, where she married a lawyer. They had one child, but both husband and child died of yellow fever. I have seen his death certificate. He left her comfortably off.

"I am a hop merchant, with a good income. When we married, we took a nice villa at Norbury. Our place is countrified—an inn, a few houses above us, and an empty cottage on the other side of a field which faces us. My wife had insisted on making over all her property to me—against my will. Two months ago she asked me for a hundred pounds of her money; I gave it to her. 'Someday I'll tell you why I need it,' she said, 'but not at present.'

"Last Monday evening, strolling across the field, I noticed a pile of rugs outside the cottage. As I walked past, I suddenly saw a face watching me from one of the upper windows. It was livid, chalky white, rigid and unnatural. Curious, I knocked at the door. A gaunt woman came out.

" 'I am your neighbor yonder,' said I. 'Can I be of help?'

" 'We'll just ask when we want ye,' said she, shutting the door.

"I said nothing of this to my wife, for she is a very nervous woman. I did mention, however, that the cottage was occupied.

"I am usually a sound sleeper, but that night I became dimly conscious that my wife had dressed to go out. The creak of the front door woke me fully, and I looked at my watch—it was three in the morning. About twenty minutes later she returned.

" 'Where in the world have you been?' I asked as she entered.

"She gave a violent start and a gasping cry when I spoke.

" 'I felt I was choking and needed fresh air,' she said.

"From her voice, I could tell what she was saying was false. We hardly exchanged a word during breakfast, and afterwards I went out for a long walk. On my way back I passed the cottage. Imagine my surprise when the door opened, and my wife came out. When she saw me, she turned white with fear.

" 'Ah, Jack,' she said, 'I came to greet our new neighbors.'

" 'So,' said I, 'this is where you went during the night.'

" 'I have not been here before,' she cried.

" 'I shall enter that cottage now, and find out the truth!'

" 'No, no, Jack, for God's sake!' she gasped. 'I implore you. I swear I will tell you everything someday. Trust me, Jack! If you force your way in, it will be all over between us!'

"There was such despair in her manner, that I relented.

" 'I will trust you on one condition,' I said. 'You must promise that there will be no more nightly visits, and that you will keep nothing from me in the future. I will forget what is past.'

" 'It shall be as you wish,' she said earnestly.

"For two days she kept her promise. On the third day, I came home from town by the 2:40 instead of the 3:36, my usual train. As I entered the house, the maid ran into the hall, startled.

" 'Where is your mistress?' I asked.

" 'I think she has gone for a walk,' she answered.

"I went upstairs to make sure my wife was not there. I happened to glance out of a window, and saw the maid running across the field towards the cottage. Then I saw my wife and the maid hurrying back. I rushed out, and ran past them. I broke into the cottage—it was deserted. Only one room, on the upper floor, was well furnished—and in it was a recent photograph of my wife!

"I came home and went into my study, too angry and hurt to talk. Before I could close the door, my wife followed me in.

" 'I am sorry I broke my promise,' she said.

" 'Tell me everything, then.'

" 'I cannot, Jack, I cannot,' she cried.

"I left the house, Mr. Holmes. That was yesterday; I have not seen her since. I cannot bear this misery—tell me what to do!"

Holmes sat silent for some time, lost in thought.

"Do you think the face at the window was a man's?" he asked at last.

"That is impossible to say," answered Grant Munro.

"Have you ever seen a photograph of her first husband?"

"No, there was a great fire in Atlanta after his death; all her papers were destroyed. The death certificate is a duplicate."

"Return to Norbury," said Holmes. "If the cottage is inhabited, wire us, and we shall be with you within an hour."

When Grant Munro had left, Holmes said, "There's blackmail in it, or I am much mistaken. The woman's first husband is in the cottage. The money and photograph were demanded by him."

The wire came at teatime; by seven Holmes and Watson were at Norbury station. Grant Munro met them, greatly agitated.

"I am going to force my way in and see for myself who is in that house," said he. "I want you both there as witnesses."

As they approached the door of the cottage, a woman stepped out of the shadows. "For God's sake, don't, Jack!" she cried.

Grant Munro pushed her aside. He rushed upstairs, followed by Holmes and Watson. In the room sat a little girl dressed in a red frock and long white gloves. Watson gave a cry of horror at her face—it was livid white, and devoid of all expression. A moment later the entire mystery was explained by a smiling Holmes.

What did Holmes do that cleared up the mystery? Can you guess?

Across

1 Industrious insects
5 Muffler
10 "Weave a circle round ___ thrice"
13 Appear on the horizon
14 Presidential candidate Stevenson
15 Jotting
16 Equal: Comb. form
17 Comes to pass
19 He wrote "Old Ironsides"
21 "___ sang 'Ring-a-rosie' . . ."
22 Greek goddess of dawn
23 Less bold
24 Large number
27 Strike with wonder
28 Company brand
32 Cricket side
33 Lippo Lippi's title
34 ___ pieces (disintegrated)
35 Baseball great
36 Confused

38 Swiss river
39 Citizen of ancient Egyptian capital
41 In ___ (under one's charge)
42 Aud.
43 Glacier pinnacle
44 Asian holiday
45 Stir
47 Professorship
49 Crag
50 Most submissive
53 Needlework
56 " . . . ___ child shall lead them"
58 All ___ and done
60 Printer's term
61 Collect gradually
62 Frazzle
63 Range of knowledge
64 Villain, in the theater
65 Confederate

Down

1 Mont Blanc's the highest one
2 Ark artificer
3 Matador's mark
4 Beamed
5 Overfeeds
6 Naval officers: Abbr.
7 ___ carte
8 ___ risk (took a chance)
9 Questionable
10 Leander's beloved
11 "___ a man who wasn't there"
12 Lichen
15 ___ valve (heart part)
18 Decorticated
20 Jan., Feb., etc.
23 Flies' nemesis
24 Plunders
25 Order ___ day
26 In search of
27 Actor Carney
29 Color of "my true love's hair"

30 Public storehouse
31 Navigation aid
33 Strike a batter out
34 Not very many
36 Mother of Joseph
37 Fate
40 Come ___ (answer in kind)
44 Jot
45 Yippee!
46 Grain beard
48 Heave ___ of relief
49 Very small
50 Cover up
51 Being: Sp.
52 Paradise
53 Serbo-Croatian
54 Brad, for example
55 "There was a little ___ "
57 March Hare's beverage
59 Pasha

Puzzle V: *The Yellow Face*

Solution and epilogue on page 146

___ ___ ___ ___ ___ ___ ___ ___ ___ ___

19 Across   18 Down   32 Across   21 Across

___ ___ ___ ___ ___ , ___ ___ ___ ___ ___ ___ ___ ___ ___ ___ ___

50 Down   56 Across   29 Down

___ ___ ___ ___ ___ ___ ___ ___ ___ ___ ___ ___ .

55 Down   4 Down   40 Down   10 Across

The "Gloria Scott"—Part 1

I have some papers here, Watson," said Sherlock Holmes, as they sat one winter's night on either side of the fire, "which may interest you. They relate to the first case I was ever involved in, the extraordinary affair of the *Gloria Scott.*"

"You arouse my curiosity," said Watson.

"During my two years at college," Holmes began, "Victor Trevor was the only friend I made, and I met him only through the accident of his bull terrier freezing on to my ankle one day. He was a hearty fellow, high-spirited.

"One summer vacation he invited me to spend a month at his father's estate in Donnithorpe. We went duck shooting and fishing, we ate well—it promised to be a very pleasant stay.

"Trevor senior was a widower; Victor was his only child. A man of little culture, old Trevor had rude strength, both physically and mentally. He had travelled far and seen much. In person, he was a thickset man with grizzled hair and keen eyes.

"One evening after dinner young Trevor began to talk of the system of observation and inference which I had already formed.

" 'What can you deduce from me?' asked old Trevor, smiling.

" 'From your callosities, you have done much digging.'

" 'Made my money at the gold fields,' said he. 'Anything else?'

" 'You have been intimately associated with someone whose initials were J. A., and whom you afterwards wanted to forget.'

"Mr. Trevor stood up, stared at me strangely, and pitched forward in a dead faint. He soon recovered, and sat up.

" 'Ah, boys,' he said, 'strong as I look, my heart is weak. Might I ask, Mr. Holmes, how you know, and how much you know?'

" 'When we were fishing,' said I, 'you bared your arm, on which had been tattooed the letters 'J. A.' From their blurred appearance, I knew efforts had been made to obliterate them.'

" 'What an eye you have,' he said with a sigh of relief.

"From that day, there was a touch of suspicion in Mr. Trevor's manner towards me. At last I became so convinced I was causing him uneasiness, that I drew my visit to a close. On my last day there, an incident occurred that presaged trouble.

"We three were sitting on the lawn, when the maid came out to say that a man who would not give his name wanted to see Trevor senior, whom he knew. Trevor asked her to bring the man round. A little wizened man in dungarees, who appeared to be a sailor, shambled over. His face was thin and brown and crafty.

" 'Why, dear me, it's Hudson,' said Trevor.

" 'Hudson it is,' said the seaman. 'Thirty years since I saw you last. Here you are in your house, and me still poor.'

" 'I haven't forgotten old times,' said Trevor. 'I shall find you a situation. Now, you can get food in the kitchen.'

" 'I'm just off a two-yearer in a tramp. I wants a rest. I thought I'd get it with you or with Mr. Beddoes.'

" 'Ah!' cried Trevor, 'you know where Mr. Beddoes is?'

" 'I know where all my old friends are,' said Hudson with a sinister smile. He slouched off after the maid to the kitchen. Trevor went inside; we found him dead drunk an hour later.

"I was not sorry to leave Donnithorpe. Then, one day in autumn, I received a wire from Victor imploring me to return. He met me at the station, grown thin and careworn. 'The governor is dying,' were his first words.

" 'What is it?' I cried, as Trevor drove us rapidly towards home.

" 'Apoplexy. I doubt if he will live. Do you remember Hudson, the sailor? We let him into the house—and we have not had a peaceful hour since. He had some power over my father—my kindly governor. The maids complained of Hudson's drinking and his vile language. His insolence to my father became unbearable to me—one day, I turned him out of the room. The next day my father asked me to apologize to him. I refused.'

" ' "My boy," said my father, "you don't know how I am placed. But you shall, Victor, come what may." He shut himself up in the study all day; through the window I could see him writing. That evening release seemed near—Hudson told us he was leaving.

" ' "I've had enough of Norfolk," said he. "I'll run down to Mr. Beddoes in Hampshire. He'll be as glad to see me as you were."

" ' "You're not going away in an unkind spirit?" asked father.

" ' "I've not had my 'pology," said he. I still refused. "Very good, mate!" he snarled as he left. "We'll see about that!"

" 'My father had begun to regain his pride, when the blow fell. Last evening he received a letter with a Fordingham postmark—a trivial and absurd message—that caused him to fall down paralyzed and unconscious. Ah, my God, it is as I feared!'

"We had reached Trevor's door just as the doctor, looking grave, came out. 'Your father was conscious for an instant before the end. He said his papers were in the Japanese cabinet.'

"My friend Trevor went upstairs; an hour later he came down, pale but composed, and handed me the fatal letter. It read:

> *The supply of game for London is going steadily up. Head-keeper Hudson, we believe, has been now told to receive all orders for fly-paper and for preservation of your hen-pheasant's life.*

"I remember that Fordingham was in Hampshire—the letter could have come from Hudson or Beddoes. To have caused so drastic a result, the message could not have been trivial to Trevor. I believed its real meaning must be hidden in a secret code. I tried reading it backwards, but it made no sense, nor did alternate words. Then, in an instant I had the key to the riddle."

Holmes had hit upon the code used in the letter. What was it?

Across

1 ____ the hills
6 Colombian city
10 ____ in the belfry
14 Companion of foremost
15 Draft animals
16 Prolific unknown writer: Abbr.
17 D-day beach
18 ". . . a ____ Garcia"
20 Drum sounds
22 Italian Mr.
23 Nope
24 Stitch over
26 Adjective for the seven capital sins
28 ____ which way
30 Brain canals
32 Unlock: Poet.
33 ". . . now mine eye ____ thee"
35 Finishes third
39 Crack in a security system
41 California-Nevada lake
43 Organic compound
44 Heroine of Daniel's sonnet sequence
46 Overcharged
48 Exclaim
49 Dame Sitwell
51 Old hat
53 Actor Howard
56 École student
58 Exclamation of surprise
59 Primary color
61 ". . . whatsoever things ____ "
65 Origin
68 Dimension or degree
69 Fatten
70 Idea: Comb. form
71 Beg the question
72 Compass points
73 Gear teeth
74 Iroquoians

Down

1 "____ a horse with wings!"
2 Peruvian capital
3 Darn!
4 Come in for ____ (participate)
5 Declarers
6 Edmond Dantès' title
7 Hew
8 Minus
9 Kind of job
10 Capture
11 Put ____ to (finish)
12 Aggregate
13 Pure white
19 Antiquing agents
21 Up to now
25 Swim ____ stream
27 Tennis star
28 Fencing sword
29 ____ scaloppine
31 One G
32 Of long standing
34 "The Ballad of ____ and West"
36 Formerly
37 News
38 On the ____ (by stealth)
40 Ukrainian capital
42 Bitter-____
45 Ornament
47 ____ sack (fired)
50 Peaceful
52 Animal chain
53 Chart
54 American ostriches
55 Tidal wave
57 Capital of Nigeria
60 Caper
62 "____, Pagliaccio . . ."
63 Inner drive
64 Gr. resistance group in WWII
66 Reservoirs of psychic energy
67 Opposite of pos.

Puzzle VI: *The "Gloria Scott"—Part 1*

Solution and epilogue on page 147

__ __ __ __ __ __ __ __ __ __ __ __ __ __ __ , __ __ __ __ __ __ __ __

28 Across   68 Across   37 Down   65 Across

__ __ __ __ __ __ __ __ __ __ __ __ , __ __ __ __ __ __ __

25 Down   14 Across   47 Down

__ __ __ __ __ __ __ __ __ __ __ __ __ __ __ __

26 Across   18 Across   32 Down

__ __ __ __ __ __ __ .

53 Across

The "Gloria Scott"—Part 2

"And did you and Victor Trevor discover the secret that Hudson held over old Mr. Trevor?" asked Watson of Sherlock Holmes.

"Yes," said Holmes. "My friend was much shaken by the real meaning of the message. 'I fear my father's secret is one of sin and shame!' he cried. He gave me the statement his father had left in the Japanese cabinet, and asked me to read it to him—he had not the courage to do so himself. It is in the form of a letter of great length addressed to Victor. Here in my hands are the very papers, and I shall read to you from them:

> *My dear son, my greatest sorrow is that you should come to blush for me. My name is not Trevor; it is James Armitage. You can understand my shock when it seemed to me that young Holmes had surprised my secret. As Armitage, I worked in a London bank, was convicted of embezzlement, and sentenced to transportation. I had taken money to pay a debt of honor—I meant to replace it. But funds I had expected did not come, and a premature audit exposed my deficit. In the year '55, at age twenty-three, I found myself a felon on the bark* Gloria Scott, *bound for Australia.*

"Trevor describes the ship," said Holmes, "as an old hulk carrying thirty-eight convicts, a crew of twenty-six, eighteen soldiers, four warders, a doctor, a chaplain, the captain and his mates. The partitions between the convicts' cells were thin. Trevor's neighbor on his right was a tall, swaggering convict named Jack Prendergast, a man of good family and great ability, who had gone wrong. Trevor goes on:

> *One night I heard a voice close to my ear. Prendergast had cut an opening in the partition. I told him I knew of his trial for fraud—the money had never been recovered. 'Where d'ye suppose the money is?' Prendergast whispered through the opening. 'Right between my finger and thumb! I have plenty, and if you have money and spread it, you can do anything!' Swearing me to secrecy, he invited me to join a plot to take over the ship, hatched by a dozen convicts before they came on board. Prendergast was their leader; the "chaplain" was really his partner in crime. 'The crew is his, body and soul—he bought 'em before they signed on.' I pointed out that the soldiers were armed. 'So shall we be, my boy,' said he. 'There's a pistol for every one of us. Speak to your mate on the left tonight; see if he is to be trusted.' I did so, and found my other neighbor to be an educated young man named Evans, who was ready to join in, as were the rest of the convicts.*

"The sham chaplain," said Holmes, "armed the convicts during his frequent visits to them. Their preparations to revolt were almost completed, when chance forced their hands. Examining a sick convict, the doctor felt the outline of a pistol at the foot of the bunk, and uttered a cry. He was immediately seized and gagged. He had left unlocked the door to the deck, and the convicts swarmed up, shooting the surprised soldiers in their way. They made for the captain's cabin, to find that the chaplain had shot him dead. Jubilantly they flocked to the stateroom. They were consuming the sherry, when there was a roar of muskets, and the room filled up with bodies and blood. Those who were still alive rushed with Prendergast to the poop, from where the soldiers had aimed through a slit to the room below. Before the soldiers could load, it was all over. Of the convicts' enemies, only the warders, the mates, and the doctor were alive. It was over their lives, writes Trevor, that a quarrel arose:

> *Evans and I, and six others, had no wish to have wanton murder on our souls. It was one thing to fight armed soldiers, another to kill captured men. Prendergast said we might take a boat and go. We were given a suit of sailor togs each, some provisions, a compass, and a chart. The* Gloria Scott *had drawn away some distance from us, when we suddenly saw black smoke shoot up from her. A few seconds later she exploded, and vanished completely. We made for the place in hope of saving survivors, but we found only one, a young seaman named Hudson. He told us that after we had left, Prendergast and his gang had killed all of our enemies but the first mate, who had loosed his bonds and dashed down to the after-hold. There they found him with a matchbox in his hand, beside an open powder barrel. Whether he struck a match, or a convict misdirected a bullet, Hudson did not know. The next day we were picked up by the brig* Hotspur, *bound for Austrialia. No word ever leaked out about the true fate of the* Gloria Scott.

"Armitage and Evans changed their names to Trevor and Beddoes," said Holmes. "In Australia they became rich; they returned to England and bought country estates. As to the sailor and Beddoes, neither of them was heard of again after the day on which the letter of warning was written. They both disappeared utterly. No complaint had been lodged with the police, so that Beddoes had mistaken a threat for the deed. The police and I have different theories about the disappearance of Hudson and Beddoes."

What was Holmes's theory about the disappearance of the two men?

Across

1 Gripes
6 Values
12 Glasses' sidepiece
13 ___ to form (behaved as was expected)
14 Thrusting sword
15 On ___ (right-and-left)
17 Numeral suffix
18 Russian open carriage
20 Take an exam, in England
21 Chump
23 Cap-___ (from head to foot)
24 Dark wood
26 Aleutian island
27 Vindictively
29 Reflective
32 Unit of absorbed nuclear energy
33 Gumshoe
34 First-rate
35 Racket
36 Italian gods
39 Beer's brother
40 "___ thou still upon Gibeon"
42 Frantic
46 The dope
47 Moonfishes
48 Clothes or tiger
50 Ab ___ (from the beginning)
51 Fall to
52 In foreign parts
54 Fed. tax agency
56 Rush pell-mell
59 ". . . the ___!" (William James's inner man)
61 Moroccan seaport
62 Vetoed
63 Let off
64 More cunning

Down

1 ___ game (wins out)
2 Forecful
3 Finial
4 Took wing
5 Sawfish's saw
6 Pedestrian
7 "Drink to me ___ . . ."
8 Football linemen: Abbr.
9 Every three: Comb. form
10 New York river
11 Vision
12 Between due and quattro
13 Demolishing
16 Eyelid inflammation
19 Express a point of view
22 Play on words
24 Actor Maurice
25 ___ of Procrustes
26 Counselor, for short
28 Emerald Isle
30 Curly cabbages
31 Jack Frost, for example
35 Caused by
36 Virginia city
37 Stool pigeon
38 Wedding words
39 From: Prefix
40 Warehouseman
41 Spanish uncle
42 Jane and John
43 Time excesses of solar over lunar years
44 Petty tyrant
45 Walked leisurely
49 ___ back (returns in thought)
52 He loved an Irish Rose
53 Satan: Scot.
55 But, to Brutus
57 Biographer's collection
58 Dir.
60 Man's name, in Mecca

Puzzle VII: *The "Gloria Scott"—Part 2*

Solution and epilogue on page 148

__ __ __ __ __ __ __ , __ __ __ __ __ __ __ __ __ __ , __ __ __ __ __ __-

25 Down   42 Down   42 Across   29 Across

__ __ __   __ __ __ __ __   __ __ __ __ __ __ __ ,

      10 Down   37 Down

__ __ __ __ __ __   __ __ __ __ __   __ __   __ __ __ __ __ __ ,

62 Across   10 Down   27 Across

__ __ __ __   __ __ __ __ __ .

4 Down   52 Across

47

The Real Holmes

*P*Was there a real Sherlock Holmes? Yes, but his name was Sir Arthur Conan Doyle. It was out of his imagination, experience, and knowledge that the most widely-known figure in English literature was created. However, there were some influences or precedents that may be made out, and some that Doyle himself acknowledged.

Both Doyle and Holmes spoke of detectives who preceded Holmes, but Doyle had a bit of fun in differentiating Holmes's views from his own. Doyle thought Edgar Allan Poe's sleuth, the Chevalier Dupin, an ingenious investigator, and some of Dupin's characteristics may be found in Holmes: Dupin was a moody pipe-smoker, and possessed the apparent ability to read people's minds.

But in *A Study in Scarlet*, Doyle had Holmes observe: "Now, in my opinion, Dupin was a very inferior fellow. . . . He had some analytical genius, no doubt; but he was by no means such a phenomenon as Poe appeared to imagine."

"Have you read Gaboriau's works?" Watson asked. "Does Lecoq come up to your idea of a detective?"

"Lecoq was a miserable bungler," said Holmes, adding that Lecoq's procedures might be made into "a textbook for detectives to teach them what to avoid."

Doyle himself had a different opinion of Émile Gaboriau's works. He admired them for the clever way Gaboriau constructed the plots involving Lecoq.

Dupin and Lecoq are fictional characters, but there was a man in real life who may be said to have been the inspiration for some of Holmes's methods. He was Dr. Joseph Bell, head of the medical school and professor of surgery at the University of Edinburgh, where Doyle had enrolled at seventeen.

Doyle was among the students who attended Bell's popular lectures in the Edinburgh Infirmary. Bell was a remarkable medical diagnostician; his students, including Doyle, were also fascinated by his quick appraisal of a patient, his ability, merely by observing, to make statements about the patient's background or habits—which the patient corroborated, to the students' delight and amazement. He would then explain how he had come to his conclusions (much as Holmes explained to Watson).

Conan Doyle was an omnivorous reader, and somewhere along the way he must have also met up with Don Quixote and Sancho Panza. Like Quixote, Holmes fought the good fight, alone but for his faithful companion.

But while Conan Doyle may have been influenced by other men or other works, it was he who produced in the remarkably perceptive, prismatic Sherlock Holmes, investigator *extraordinaire*, an immortal character of his own.

The Real Watson

*P*The masked King of Bohemia arrives at the door of 221B Baker Street to see Sherlock Holmes about a confidential matter. Dr. Watson is visiting Holmes, and, having been told of the secret nature of the king's visit, prepares to leave before the king enters. Holmes detains him. "Stay where you are," says Holmes. "I am lost without my Boswell."

When Conan Doyle created Dr. John H. Watson to be the narrator of the Holmes stories, he was most likely influenced by his high regard for Boswell and *The Life of Samuel Johnson,* and he had Watson emulate Boswell both in his great admiration for the man he was writing about and in his assiduous recording of many aspects of his hero's life.

Although Watson's attention was focused on Holmes and his adventures, in the course of the saga Watson also clearly revealed aspects of his own character: he was intensely loyal to Holmes, an understanding friend, genial, reliable, retaining much of his military training, but, of course, obtuse when it came to spotting clues or discerning motives. Omit the lack of perception, and this description of Watson could well be that of a Major Wood, who was secretary to Conan Doyle for many years.

Some of Doyle's biographers, including his son Adrian, are convinced that Major Wood was the model on whom Doyle based the later development of Watson's character—although Doyle himself never said so. Wood was an efficient, loyal secretary; among other duties, he handled the voluminous mail coming to Doyle, and was trusted to cull items that he thought would interest Doyle.

Watson also resembled Major Wood physically. As the Holmes stories were told by Watson, no word picture of Watson was drawn until Doyle had Inspector Lestrade inadvertently supply one in "The Adventure of Charles Augustus Milverton." In that story, Holmes and Watson, wearing masks, had broken into blackmailer Milverton's home one night to rifle his safe on behalf of one of Holmes's clients. Holmes had just succeeded in cracking the safe, when a noise sent him and Watson darting behind a window curtain. From their hiding place they witnessed the killing of Milverton by one of his victims, who then fled. Holmes threw the entire contents of the safe into the fireplace, and he and Watson, who was almost caught, escaped over the garden wall just as the police, summoned by Milverton's household, arrived. The next day, Inspector Lestrade called on Holmes to tell about the case and ask for his help.

"The first fellow was a bit too active," said Lestrade, "but the second was caught by the under-gardener, and only got away after a struggle. He was a middle-sized, strongly built man—square jaw, thick neck, moustache, a mask over his eyes."

"That's rather vague," said Holmes. "Why, it might be a description of Watson!" It was also a description of Major Wood.

The Musgrave Ritual

S herlock Holmes dragged from his bedroom a large tin box containing bundles of his early cases. Watson had just suggested that he lessen the sitting-room clutter by stowing away records of his later ones. But instead of putting anything into the box, Holmes lifted out a piece of paper and three small metal discs.

"Relics," said he, "of the adventure of the Musgrave Ritual."

"I should be glad," said Watson, "to hear about it."

"And leave the litter as it is?" asked Holmes, smiling. "To begin, when I first came up to London I had rooms in Montague Street, and it was there that Reginald Musgrave, whom I had known at college, called on me. He was a tall, thin man, scion of one of the oldest families in the country, whose Manor House of Hurlstone is the oldest inhabited one in western Sussex.

" 'Since my father's death two years ago,' said he, 'I have had Hurlstone to manage. But I understand that you are turning to practical ends those powers with which you used to amaze us. Your advice would be most welcome. Lately we have had strange doings at Hurlstone, and the police have been unable to help.'

" 'Pray let me have the details,' I said eagerly.

" 'I am a bachelor,' said Musgrave, 'but I keep a large staff of servants— Hurlstone is a rambling place. The servant who has been with us longest is Brunton, the butler. He is an intelligent, handsome man of forty, but he has one fault—since his wife died he has become a Don Juan. A few months ago he became engaged to Rachel Howells, our second maid, but has since thrown her over for another. Rachel, an excitable girl, had a sharp touch of brain fever, and has gone about—until yesterday—like a shadow of her former self. That was our first drama.

" 'One night last week—on Thursday—I found myself unable to sleep, and decided to go down to the library. I was surprised to see a glimmer of light from the open door. I crept up and peeped in. Brunton was sitting at a table, looking at a map. As I watched, he rose, walked to a bureau, took from it a paper, brought it to the table, and began to study it minutely. I took a step forward; Brunton looked up, and sprang to his feet, livid with fear. He snatched up his map, and thrust it into his pocket.

" ' "So!" I said. "You will leave my service tomorrow!"

" 'He slunk past me without a word. I picked up the paper he had taken from the bureau—a copy of the questions and answers in the Musgrave Ritual, which each Musgrave for centuries has gone through on coming of age. It is of no practical use. As I turned to go, I found Brunton standing before me. Pleading that he could not bear the disgrace, he begged me to let him resign and leave in a month. I agreed, but only to a week.

" 'Three days later, Brunton failed to appear after breakfast for the day's instructions. As I left the dining room, I met Rachel Howells. She looked pale and wan. I told her to return to her room downstairs, and asked her to send Brunton up.

" ' "The butler is gone," she said. She fell back against the wall, shrieking with hysterical laughter. Horrified, I rang for help. She was taken to her room, and I searched for Brunton—in vain. His bed had not been slept in, and his black suit and slippers were missing. I called in the local police, but without success. Rain had fallen, and there were no clues to be found.

" 'A few days after Brunton disappeared, the nurse who had been hired to look after Rachel Howells nodded off, and woke to find her gone. Her footmarks were traced to the edge of the lake. Dragging the lake did not yield the poor girl's body, but, oddly, a linen bag containing some rusted metal and several dull-colored pebbles. The county police are at their wits' end.'

" 'The girl had gone to the lake to throw in the linen bag,' I said. 'I must see this paper Brunton risked his place for.'

" 'I have a copy with me,' said Musgrave. 'The original has no date, but the spelling is of the mid-seventeenth century.'

"It is the very paper I have here, Watson. I will read the questions and answers to you as they stand:

Whose was it?
His who is gone.
Who shall have it?
He who will come.
Where was the sun?
Over the oak.
Where was the shadow?
Under the elm.
How was it stepped?
North by ten and by ten, east by five and by five, south by two and by two,
west by one and by one, and so under.
What shall we give for it?
All that is ours.
Why should we give it?
For the sake of the trust.

"'Excuse me, Musgrave,' I said after reading the ritual, 'but your butler had more insight than ten generations of his masters. He must have seen this more than once. It may lead us to Brunton and the girl. Let's visit Hurlstone to find the oak and the elm.'

"We were at Hurlstone that same afternoon. The famous L-shaped building had the date 1607 chiselled on it. In front of it stood a patriarch among oaks; a huge old elm some distance away had been struck down by lightning, but Musgrave knew its height—sixty-four feet—and its location. When the sun was just grazing the top of the oak, I placed a six-foot rod at the site of the elm

" 'A patriarch among oaks.' "

and measured its shadow, from which I calculated the length of the elm's shadow. In this way I was able to fix the exact spot to start pacing off the steps. Imagine my disappointment when they led me finally two paces down a stone-flagged passage of the house. But, fortunately, Musgrave checked my calculations.

" 'You have omitted the "and so under!" ' he cried.

"I had thought that it meant we were to dig, but now I saw that I was wrong. 'Is there a cellar under this?' I asked.

" 'Yes, and as old as the house. Here, through this door.'

"We went down to the old cellar, and in the middle of it lay a large, heavy flatstone with a rusted iron ring in its center; attached to the ring was a thick shepherd's-check muffler.

" 'By Jove!' cried Musgrave. 'That's Brunton's muffler.'

"I tugged at the muffler, but could not move the stone. We summoned a burly constable, and with his help I removed it. A small chamber lay open beneath us. At one side was a brass-bound wooden box, the lid of which was hinged open. Small metal discs lay at the bottom of the box—nothing else. At the moment we gave the box no thought—our eyes were riveted on the figure of a man crouching beside it. When we drew the body up, Musgrave recognized his missing butler. He had been dead some days, but there was no wound or bruise to show how he had met his end.

"What had the family concealed with such elaborate precautions? What part had the girl Howells played in the matter? I sat down on a keg in the corner of the cellar to think it over.

"Brunton had correctly interpreted the ritual and had found the cellar. But the flagstone was too heavy for a man to move unaided. He could not risk bringing help in from outside. Whom could he ask inside the house? Rachel Howells had once loved him. He would make his peace with her. But for the two of them, and one a woman, it must have been heavy work, raising that stone. What could they do? Probably, as they dragged the stone up, they thrust chunks of wood into the chink until the opening was large enough to crawl through, and then they held it open with a piece placed lengthwise. I had noticed just such pieces of wood on the floor of the cellar.

"Only one person could fit into the hole—the girl must have waited above. Brunton let himself down, opened the box, handed up its contents—and then, what happened? The man who had wronged Rachel Howells was in her power. Was it chance that the wood slipped, or not? No matter, here was the secret of her blanched face and shaken nerves. But what had been in the box? Of course, the old metal and pebbles dragged from the lake!

"Musgrave interrupted my thoughts. 'These are the coins of Charles the First,' said he, holding out the small metal discs.

" 'Let me see the contents of the linen bag!' I cried.

"We ascended to his study, where I examined the metal and pebbles. I rubbed one of the pebbles on my sleeve, and it glowed in my hand. The metal work was a double ring, bent and twisted out of shape.

" 'My ancestor, Sir Ralph Musgrave, was a prominent cavalier, and right-hand man of Charles the Second,' said Musgrave.

" 'Ah, indeed,' I said. 'I must congratulate you on coming into the possession, though in a tragic manner, of a relic of great intrinsic and historical value.'

" 'What is it, then?' gasped Musgrave in astonishment."

Can you deduce, from the clues, Holmes's answer to Musgrave?

Across

1 Put the finishing touch on
6 Indian prince
10 Filly, for example
14 Oblivion
15 Algerian seaport
16 Caen's river
17 Traveling salesman
18 French SSTs
20 Egg drink
21 Price rise
23 Metal bars
24 Earth's pull
26 Ancient Asian
27 Black cuckoo
28 Producing motion
31 Backs out
34 Bankbook benefits: Abbr.
35 ___ up (dress)
37 Alda or Arkin
38 Preparation, for short
39 ". . . the ___, the yellow leaf"
40 Job: Slang
41 For men only
43 George Washington's portraitist
45 Classifies
47 Upsilon follower
48 Kimono sashes
49 ___ a Salesman
53 Feline's fancy
56 Cut: Brit.
57 Associate of CIO
58 "The stately homes ___!"
60 Lone Ranger's sidekick
62 "Black as the Pit from ___ . . ."
63 Dash!
64 Novelist Walpole, et al.
65 Waste allowance
66 Lethargic
67 Letters from the Greek *sigma*

Down

1 Trolley-bell sound
2 Harshness
3 The end
4 Mariner's direction
5 ". . . ___ but the truth"
6 Wobbly
7 Indonesian islands
8 Winter mo.
9 Kind of history
10 Put out of mind
11 Church calendar
12 Dill
13 "Not that I loved Caesar___ . . ."
19 French waves
22 Inflammation of: Suffix
25 Worthless
26 Chinese dynasty
28 Companions of cabbages
29 Shrub genus
30 Pen pal, for short
31 Kid
32 Charles Lamb
33 Ponies
36 Give the business
38 Makes fine lace
39 Please
41 Edna Ferber novel
42 Hit a three-bagger
43 Gush forth
44 "Be she fairer ___ day"
46 Shakespearean poem
49 Pop
50 ___ out at (frequents)
51 Bottom ___ sea
52 *The Mill on the* ___
53 Egyptian Christian
54 ___ effort
55 From a distance: Comb. form
56 Cold-weather spell
59 "Long, Long ___"
61 Ending for danger or peril

Puzzle VIII: *The Musgrave Ritual*

1	2	3	4	5		6	7	8	9		10	11	12	13
14						15					16			
17						18			19					
20				21	22				23					
24			25					26						
			27				28					29	30	
31	32	33				34						35		36
37					38					39				
40				41	42				43	44				
	45		46					47						
			48				49				50	51	52	
53	54	55				56					57			
58					59				60	61				
62				63					64					
65				66					67					

Solution and epilogue on page 149

"___ ___ ___ ___ ___ ___ ___ ___ ___ ___ ___ ___ ___ ___ ___

22 Down   5 Down   13 Down   44 Down

___ ___ ___ ___ ___ ___ ___ ___ ___ ___ ___ ___ ___

9 Down   1 Across   51 Down   43 Across

___ ___ ___ ___ ___ ___ ___ ___ ."

28 Down   58 Across

The Adventure of the Solitary Cyclist

Late on a Saturday evening in April of '95, a tall and beautiful young woman named Violet Smith presented herself at Baker Street, and implored Sherlock Holmes's assistance. He was deeply immersed in important research at the time, and Watson watched with interest to see if he would accede to her plea. In his gallant way Holmes asked her to take a seat, and to inform Watson and himself of her trouble. She told them a most curious story.

"When my father died, my mother and I were left poor and alone, except for my uncle, Ralph Smith, who went to Africa twenty-five years ago. We were most excited when we saw, last December, a lawyer's advertisement in *The Times* inquiring for our whereabouts. Hoping we had come into a fortune, we went to his office, and there we met two gentlemen, Mr. Robert Carruthers and Mr. Woodley, who were on a visit from South Africa. They said my uncle, who had died some months before in great poverty in Johannesburg, had asked his friends to see that my mother and I were not in want.

"Mr. Woodley was a most odious person, a coarse, red-moustached young man, who kept making eyes at me. I was sure that my fiancé Cyril Morton would not wish me to know such a person. Mr. Carruthers, a much older man, was more agreeable. He was a dark, clean-shaven, silent person. He suggested that I come to Chiltern Grange, the place he had rented near Farnham, and teach music to his only daughter, aged ten. He said that I might go home to stay with my mother on weekends. I accepted his offer of a hundred a year. Mr. Carruthers was a widower, and had engaged Mrs. Dixon, a respectable woman, as housekeeper. The child was a dear, and I enjoyed my work, until Mr. Woodley came for a week's visit.

"Mr. Woodley's behavior towards me was most offensive. He tried to make love to me, boasted of his wealth, said that if I married him, I would own diamonds, and finally, one day, he seized me in his arms. Mr. Carruthers had to tear him from me, whereupon he knocked Mr. Carruthers down, and that was the end of his visit.

"Every Saturday, Mr. Holmes, I bicycle six miles to Farnham Station to get the 12:22 to town. One spot on the road from Chiltern Grange is very lonely; it lies for a mile between Charlington Heath on one side and the woods round Charlington Hall on the other. Two weeks ago, as I passed this place, I looked over my shoulder and saw, two hundred yards behind me, a middle-aged man with a short, dark beard, also on a bicycle. I looked back before I reached Farnham, and he was gone. On my return on Monday, I saw the same man on the same stretch of road. The incident occurred again the following Saturday and Monday. I mentioned it to Mr. Carruthers, and he ordered a horse and trap so that in the future I would have a companion going with me to and from the station.

"The trap was not delivered this week, so I had to cycle again. When I came to Charlington Heath, there behind me was the man. To see his face more clearly, I slowed down my machine, but he slowed down his. There is a sharp turning of the road, so I rode quickly round it and waited. As he did not appear, I looked round the turn. I could see a mile of road, but he was not on it. To make it more extraordinary, there was no side road at this point down which he could have cycled."

"Then he must have taken a footpath toward Charlington Hall," said Holmes. "Where is the gentlemen to whom you are engaged?"

"He is an engineer in Coventry—I should have recognized him."

"Have you any other admirers?"

"Several before I knew Cyril. Mr. Woodley, if you can call him one. And I feel that Mr. Carruthers takes a great deal of interest in me, although he is a perfect gentleman."

"What does he do for a living?"

"I understand he is rich. He goes to the city several times a week, and is interested in South African gold shares."

"Yet he has no carriages or horses. Let me know any fresh developments, Miss Smith. In the meantime, I shall make inquiries."

After she had gone, Holmes said, "First, we must find out who are the tenants of Charlington Hall. Then, the connection between Carruthers and Woodley, and why Carruthers pays double the wage for a governess. I am too busy; I call on you, Watson."

Arriving at Farnham Station Monday morning, Watson quickly found the scene of Miss Smith's adventure. On one side of the road lay the heath, and on the other a yew hedge surrounded the wooded park of Charlington Hall. The hedge was broken by the gateway to the Hall, and by several gaps which led into footpaths. Watson hid behind a clump of gorse in the heath, and watched as the mysterious cyclist came from the direction of Chiltern Grange, sprang from his bicycle, and disappeared through a gap in the hedge. A quarter of an hour later Miss Smith cycled past on her way to the Grange, and was followed almost at once by the man. Presently the man rode back, turned in at the gate, and cycled toward the Hall.

The Farnham house agent referred Watson to a London firm for information about Charlington Hall. There he learned that the Hall had been rented a month ago to a Mr. Williamson, an elderly man.

Sherlock Holmes was not happy with Watson's report. "You went to a London agent to find out about Charlington Hall's tenants!"

"What should I have done?" cried Watson, with some heat.

"Gone to the nearest public house for gossip. Elderly Williamson is not our active cyclist. We can do little until Saturday."

The next morning Holmes had a note from Miss Smith, reporting that Carruthers had proposed marriage, which she of course had refused; the air was strained. Holmes decided to go to Farnham that afternoon. He returned with a cut lip and a lump on his forehead.

"I used my boxing skills today, Watson," said Holmes, smiling. "The landlord at the pub told me that Mr. Williamson is a white-bearded man, rumored to be a clergyman, who lives alone at the Hall. I have since made inquiries at a clerical agency; there *was* a man of that name in orders, whose career has been a dark one. The landlord also told me that Woodley was a constant visitor at the Hall, and there were others—'a warm lot, sir.' Then, who should walk in but Woodley himself; he had been in the tap room and had heard the whole conversation. What did I mean by asking questions? He gave me a vicious backhander, but the next few minutes were delicious. I emerged as you see; Woodley went home in a cart."

Thursday brought another letter from Miss Smith. This time she said that she would be leaving Carruthers's employ on Saturday, due to the presence of an angry Woodley at the Grange once more. Carruthers had got a trap, so the road presented no dangers.

"But I fear for Miss Violet," said Holmes. "I think we both must go down to Farnham on Saturday to see to her safety."

Saturday morning was bright and clear. Walking toward Chiltern Grange, Holmes and Watson could see from a rise in the road a vehicle moving in their direction. Holmes gave an exclamation of impatience. "If that is her trap, I am afraid that she will be past Charlington before we can meet her. I have not allowed for a margin of time in case she made for an earlier train!"

When they had passed the rise, they could no longer see the vehicle. A few minutes later, an open carriage, empty, the horse cantering, the reins trailing, suddenly appeared round the curve of the road and rattled towards them. "It's abduction, Watson!" cried Holmes. "Jump in, and let's see if we can repair my blunder."

Holmes turned the horse round, and they flew back along the road. As they turned the curve, the stretch of road between the Hall and the heath opened up. Watson grasped Holmes's arm.

"That's the man!" he gasped.

A bearded man was cycling furiously toward them. He sprang from his machine, shouting, "Stop there! Stop! Where did you get that carriage?" He drew a revolver from his pocket. Holmes pulled up, threw the reins to Watson, and jumped down.

"Where is Miss Violet Smith?" Holmes demanded.

"You're in her carriage! You ought to know where she is!"

"We met the carriage on the road—there was no one in it. We drove back to help the young lady."

"Good Lord! They've got her, that hellhound Woodley and the blackguard parson. Stand by me and we'll save her!" the stranger cried. He ran towards a gap in the hedge, with Holmes and Watson following. "This is where they came through. See the footmarks! Halloa, who's this in the bush?"

A young fellow about seventeen lay on his back, a terrible cut on his head. He was insensible, but alive. "That's Peter, the groom," cried the stranger.

" 'It's abduction, Watson!' "

"He drove her. Let him lie—we may save her from the worst fate that can befall a woman!"

They ran frantically down the path, until they reached the shrubbery which surrounded the house. Suddenly, a woman's shrill scream burst from the thick clump of bushes in front of them. They broke through, into a glade circled with trees. Standing under an oak were three people—Violet Smith, drooping and faint, a handkerchief round her mouth; opposite her, brutal, red-moustached Woodley, waving a riding crop; between them, gray-bearded Williamson, wearing a short surplice, who had evidently just completed a wedding service, for he pocketed his prayer book and slapped Woodley on the back in congratulation.

"I know who you are," said Woodley to the stranger. "You and your pals have come just in time to meet Mrs. Woodley."

1) What did the stranger do in response to Woodley's statement, and 2) what did he say?

59

Across

1 U. S. gastronomic guru
6 Experts
10 Book of the Bible
14 Rose oil
15 Instrument with 46 strings
16 Small case
17 Nettle plant
18 Celtic language
19 Delivery trucks
20 ". . . and ___ as the rose"
22 Intersect
24 Those: Sp.
25 Science of life: Abbr.
26 Exchanges
29 Butchers' tools
33 Attila was one
34 Spacecraft rocket
36 Field fortification
37 School subj.
39 Quiver of arrows

41 City on the Truckee
42 Not, in Nuremberg
44 "Hitch your wagon to ___"
46 Manicure the lawn
47 Contestants
49 French auto-race city
51 Chemical suffixes
52 Voyaging
53 Peddles
55 Author of *The Old Wives' Tale*
59 Philippine knife
60 Wynken, Blynken, and Nod, for example
63 ___ incognita
64 Patron saint of Norway
65 Burden
66 Incite
67 Kind of tea
68 TV award
69 ___ with (is one's responsibility)

Down

1 Cutting remark
2 Etc.
3 Vapor: Comb. form
4 ___ the roof (whooped it up)
5 Bureau
6 Attention-getting coughs
7 Elevator cage
8 Vocalized pauses
9 Hard money
10 Turner
11 Namesakes of actress Hagen
12 Wine casks
13 ". . . frets ___ hour upon the stage"
21 Desert gardens
23 Bellow
25 Puff up
26 Macbeth's title
27 Quarrel
28 Put on ___ (sham)
29 Salad ingredient

30 Dropsy
31 Talked away
32 Flatters: Slang
35 "___ all there is . . ."
38 Recovered from
40 Dishonest
43 Cooler
45 Set foot in again
48 Settle down snugly
50 Horsemanship
52 In ___ (collectively)
53 ___ up (hide out)
54 Wings
56 Units of work
57 Turkey or fox
58 Beige, ecru, etc.
59 Fishing-line float
61 Gypsy man
62 "___ the master of my fate"

Puzzle IX:
The Adventure of the Solitary Cyclist

Solution and epilogue on page 150

1)__ __ __ __ __   __ __ __ __   __ __ __ __ __ __   __ __ __ __ __ ,
  38 Down   13 Down   40 Down   1 Across

__ __ __ __ __ __   __ __ __   __ __ __ __ __ __ __ .   2) " __ __ __
 4 Down   13 Down   10 Down   62 Down

__ __   __ __ __ __ __ __ __ __ __ __ !"
59 Down   7 Down   10 Across   8 Down

Professor Moriarty (Sss!!)

P "Tall and thin. . . . pale and ascetic-looking." Almost a mirror image of Sherlock Holmes, but for the dome-like forehead and the sunken eyes. An intellect as great as Holmes's, a phenomenal mathematical faculty. What turned Professor Moriarty into the "Napoleon of crime"?

Sherlock Holmes believed that criminal tendencies were inherited—an evil strain in the blood. In Moriarty's case, the tendencies combined with extraordinary mental powers to create one of the world's most fiendish criminals.

Moriarty became incalculably rich through his machinations, but he came by his professorial title honestly. As a young man he had written a mathematical treatise that had won him a chair at a university. But a brilliant academic career was cut short when he was forced by "dark rumors" to resign. He came to London, set up as a mathematical coach, and embarked on his diabolical new career as the invisible, organizing power of a vast criminal network.

"The man pervades London, and no one has heard of him," Holmes cried to Watson. Holmes's deep horror at Moriarty's crimes was sometimes lost in admiration of Moriarty's skill in concealing himself behind a cloak of respectability. The inspectors at Scotland Yard thought Holmes a bit balmy on the subject of Moriarty—their investigations revealed only a scholarly gentleman.

As Holmes was the great consulting detective, so Moriarty was the great consultant in crime. But while Holmes took an active role in combating evil, Moriarty did little but plan his nefarious crimes, "sitting motionless like a spider in the centre of its web." His large organization carried out the commission of the crimes, and also passed word to him when there was evil to be done. So ingeniously did Moriarty lay his plans, that his agents were rarely caught; if one was apprehended, the professor supplied money for his bail and defense—he himself remained undetected.

If Moriarty was so shadowy as to be invisible, how did Sherlock Holmes learn of him? Though Moriarty was, by Holmes's own admission, his intellectual equal, there was a significant difference between them. It lay in Holmes's superior insight, and in his understanding of the way of the world. He *deduced* Moriarty's existence. He had become aware that hidden behind much of the crime in London was a malignant brain of great organizing ability.

Determined to uncover the monster, Holmes at last succeeded in finding "a thread" that led him to Moriarty. Faced with Scotland Yard's incompetence, he set out on his own to collect evidence against Moriarty, but the wily villain knew of Holmes's every move. The whole tale is told in "The Final Problem," a story Conan Doyle wrote to finish Holmes off—Doyle wanted to devote his time to writing historical novels. Moriarty had been created by Doyle in "The Final Problem" expressly to do Holmes in. Doyle chose to obliterate them both by having Watson report his belief that the two men, locked in a death struggle on the brink of the towering Reichenbach Falls, had reeled into the roaring abyss to vanish forever.

Years later, when public sentiment at last induced Doyle to bring Holmes back to life, Doyle had no difficulty in explaining how his hero had escaped death, while Moriarty had perished. Doyle had drawn Holmes as the complete Renaissance man, skilled not only in the arts and sciences, but also in the manly arts of self-defense. Moriarty was no match for such a man. At the Reichenbach Falls, Holmes had used his knowledge of Japanese wrestling to slip out of Moriarty's grasp, as the archvillain fell to his doom.

The giant figure of Professor Moriarty appears in only one of the sixty Holmes stories, and is talked about or hinted at in only six others. Conan Doyle must surely have used black magic to create so unforgettable a villain in so small a space.

Professor Moriarty.

The Adventure of the Priory School—Part 1

On the morning of May 17th the large pompous figure of Thorneycroft Huxtable, Ph. D., founder of the select Priory School, staggered into the sitting room at Baker Street and fell insensible to the floor. Revived by Sherlock Holmes and Dr. Watson, he said, "You must come with me to Mackleton. The Duke of Holdernesse's only son has disappeared."

On May 1st, he went on, the Duke's secretary, James Wilder, had enrolled ten-year-old Lord Arthur Saltire at his school. The boy had been unhappy at Holdernesse Hall since his mother had left the Duke to live in France. Early morning, May 14th, Arthur was missed from his second-floor room. His bed had been slept in; he had dressed fully. His window was open, but the ivy showed no signs of descent.

A search had uncovered another disappearance—that of Heidegger, the German master, whose room, also on the second floor, faced the same way as Arthur's. His bed, too, had been slept in, but he had left without shirt or socks, letting himself down by the ivy. His bicycle was missing.

"Three days wasted before you came here! Why?" asked Holmes.

"The police were called in, but without result. Yet his Grace wants no one else involved—I came to you in my despair."

"Was any other bicycle missing? Did Lord Saltire have any visitors or letters the day before he disappeared?"

"No other bicycle was missing. Arthur had had no callers, and only one letter—it was addressed in the Duke's stiff handwriting. We do not have the letter; the boy took it with him."

"Has he ever had a letter from France? No? But you indicated that his sympathies were with his mother. How do you know?"

"I have had some confidential talks with James Wilder."

Holmes, Watson, and Dr. Huxtable were soon bound for Mackleton. At the school, they found the tall, thin Duke and dapper young Wilder waiting angrily—they had heard of Huxtable's plan to see Holmes.

"His Grace still has faith in the police!" said Wilder.

"But since you are here, Mr. Holmes," said the Duke, "I welcome your help, and should be pleased if you will stay at the Hall."

"I thank your Grace, but I will remain at the scene of the mystery. Excuse me, sir, but do you think the Duchess is involved? Also, may I ask if you have had any demands for ransom?"

"I have had no demands for money. The Duchess is not involved, but possibly the lad fled to her, aided and abetted by the German."

"Did you post your last letter to your son yourself?"

"The Duke does not post letters," said Wilder. "I do that."

Soon after the Duke and Wilder departed, Sherlock Holmes left the school; he returned late, with an ordnance map of the area.

"Look, Watson. The square near the bottom is the Priory School. The High Road under it runs past, east and west, with no side road for a mile either way.

At the east crossroad a constable told me no one had passed by on the night in question. To the west is the Red Bull Inn; the landlady had sent for a doctor and spent the night watching the road for him. No one had passed. South of the High Road are small fields, with stone walls between them—a bicycle is impossible. Just north of the school is a lawn, then small woods called the Ragged Shaw. Then Lower Gill Moor stretches ten miles to Holdernesse Hall, a mile east of which is the Fighting Cock Inn."

There was a knock at Watson's door, and an excited Dr. Huxtable entered. "Look here, Arthur's cap! Gypsies found it on the moor!"

Early next morning Holmes and Watson struck across the moor until they came to a green belt of morass that lay in its middle.

"In this dry weather," said Holmes, "our best chance of finding bicycle tracks is here. You can see tracks of sheep and cows."

They came to a ribbon of pathway. And there was the track of a bicycle leading away from the school—but the wrong track!

"This was made by a Dunlop tire with a patch," said Holmes. "Last night I learned that Heidegger's tires were Palmers."

They were able to find traces of the track back to the Ragged Shaw, whence it started. Returning to the morass, they came at last on Heidegger's cycle tracks, with stains of blood upon them.

"Bad!" said Holmes. "Stand clear, Watson! Strange, no other tracks here but that of cows on this side path. Let us push on."

They found Heidegger's body near some gorse bushes. Seeing a peasant, Holmes dispatched him with a note to Huxtable, and mused to Watson about the case. He had examined the boy's window; the lad *had* gone down by the ivy, and by his own will. Heidegger had left at short notice, evidently having seen the boy's flight and gone in pursuit. The lad did not have the strength to kill Heidegger—he *must* have had a companion. Yet—only cow tracks!

The Dunlop tracks had pointed to the Fighting Cock. At the inn, Holmes tested the surly landlord, Reuben Hayes, by asking for a bicycle to get to the Hall, as he had news of the Duke's lost son.

"What, you're on his track?" asked Hayes, visibly startled.

"He's been in Liverpool, and is expected here at any hour."

Turning suddenly genial, Hayes said, "I was the Dook's coachman, and he treated me cruel, but I wish him no harm."

Holmes and Watson, famished, went into the kitchen to eat. Left alone by Hayes, Holmes looked out a window which opened on to a courtyard. In the far corner was a grimy smithy.

Suddenly Holmes cried, "By heavens, Watson, I've got it! Remember the cow tracks on the moor? They were everywhere. And how many cows did we see? None! And the tracks—" He arranged bread crumbs on the table. "Some were like this"—::::—"and some like this"—:.:.:.:.—"and some like this"—.·.·.·.·—

"And what do you deduce from that?" asked Watson.

What did Holmes have to say about the cow tracks on the moor?

Across

1 Easy as falling off ____
5 Love seats
10 Spill the beans
14 One of the three Roman Fates
15 What one?
16 Roof edge
17 Attractive person: Slang
18 Braids
20 Schweitzer's *Out of* ____ *and Thought*
22 Seesaws
23 Food fragment
24 King with a golden touch
25 Sweeping blow
28 Twitch
29 Tendon
33 ____ the road (leaves)
34 My, in Montmartre
35 Eye membrane
36 "____ live and breathe!"
37 Rides at an easy pace

39 Kind of lace
40 Dealt in used cars
42 Yeas
43 Poop or flight
44 Fall in folds
45 Eisenhower
46 Propensities
47 Get out of
49 The Cape
50 Red or Revolution
53 Outcries
56 Extraordinary
58 Stylish
60 ". . . ____ for all seasons"
61 Miss Kett of the comics, et al.
62 Poi source
63 Spectrum stripe
64 Enlists again: Mil. slang
65 Goulash

Down

1 ____ so forth
2 Weaving machine
3 Exclusively
4 Rides hard
5 Chimney bird
6 Without, in Weimar
7 In good health
8 Vinegary
9 Tatter
10 Makes oneself scarce
11 Spike, as a drink
12 State positively
13 "____, the landlord's daughter"
19 Rent contracts
21 Choler
24 Slip-up
25 Pottery fragment
26 "A sadder and a ____ man"
27 "____ far, far better thing . . ."
28 Basis of decimal system
30 Actor David

31 Make into law
32 "She ____ in beauty . . ."
34 Kind of money
35 B. & O. and U. P.
37 Quick-witted
38 Hurricane center
41 ____ -shut-case
43 Subtracts
45 Imagine
46 Sound of derision
48 Questioner
49 Karpov's game
50 Grouser
51 Blood: Comb. form.
52 "____ old cowhand . . ."
53 Rebuff
54 ____ is (in other words)
55 Forefather
57 Measure of heat: Abbr.
59 Intimidate

Puzzle X:
The Adventure of the Priory School—Part 1

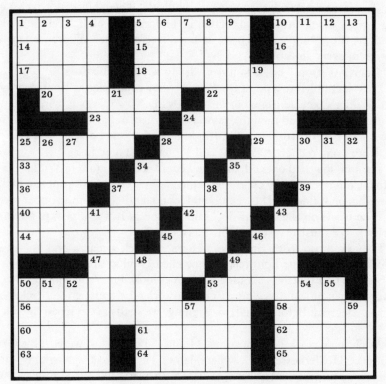

Solution and epilogue on page 151

Solution and epilogue on page 151

"— — — — — — — — — — — — — — — — — — — -

3 Down   54 Down   27 Down   56 Across

— — — — — — — — — — — — — — — — —,

59 Down   15 Across   32 Down

— — — — — — —, — — — — — — — — — —."

37 Across   1 Down   4 Down

The Adventure of the Priory School—Part 2

On their way back to the Fighting Cock, Holmes and Watson had turned off the road and were going up a hillside, when they saw a cyclist coming swiftly along from the direction of Holdernesse Hall. Hiding behind a boulder, they glimpsed the pale, agitated face of James Wilder—a face with horror in every lineament.

"Come, Watson," cried Holmes, "let us see what he does!"

They scrambled to a point from where they could see the front door of the inn. Wilder's bicycle leaned against the wall. No one was moving about the house. Dusk fell, and then they saw a trap wheel out of the yard and into the road, and ride off furiously towards the nearby town of Chesterfield.

"It was not Wilder in flight," said Holmes. "There he is."

The inn door had opened, and they could see the figure of Wilder peering into the night, evidently expecting someone. A second figure approached, the door shut on Wilder and his visitor, and soon a lamp was lit in an upper room.

"The bar is on the other side," said Holmes. "It was a private guest who arrived. We must investigate this more closely."

They crept up to the inn door. Holmes struck a match and held it near Wilder's bicycle—its light fell on a patched Dunlop tire.

Standing on Watson's shoulders, Holmes looked into the lighted room. He leaped down quickly, saying, "Come, my friend. I must go to Mackleton to send a telegram. Before tomorrow evening, we shall have reached the solution to the mystery."

At eleven o'clock next morning, Holmes and Watson were in his Grace's study at Holdernesse Hall, where James Wilder was apologizing for the Duke's inability to see them—he had been made ill by the tragic news of Heidegger's death, about which Dr. Huxtable had wired. But Holmes was adamant. After an hour, the Duke appeared. The nobleman, holder of a vast estate, a former cabinet minister, looked haggard and tormented, older than the day before.

Holmes asked that Wilder leave the room, so that he could speak more freely. The request being granted, Holmes said, "I should like you to confirm Dr. Huxtable's assurance to Dr. Watson and myself that a reward has been offered in this case—£5000 to anyone who will tell you where your son is, and £1000 for the name or names of those who keep him in custody."

"Exactly," said the Duke.

"Then please make out a check to me for £6000."

"Is this a joke, Mr. Holmes?"

"Not at all, your Grace. I was never more earnest in my life. I know where your son is, and who is holding him."

"Where is he?" the Duke gasped. "And whom do you accuse?"

"He is at the Fighting Cock Inn. And I accuse you."

The Duke clawed the air with his hands, like one sinking into an abyss.

Then, with an effort, he sat down and bowed his head.

"I saw you together last night," said Holmes.

"Does anyone else beside your friend here know?"

"I have spoken to no one."

"I am about to write your check. I assume that you and Dr. Watson are men of discretion, Mr. Holmes. If only you two know of the incident, it need not go any further. I think £12,000 is the sum I owe you, is it not?"

"I fear, your Grace, that matters cannot be arranged so easily. There is the death of the schoolmaster to be accounted for."

"But James knew nothing of that. It was the work of the ruffian whom he had the misfortune to employ."

"When a man embarks upon a crime," said Holmes, "he is morally guilty of any other crime which may spring from it."

"But surely not in the eyes of the law," said the Duke. "James was so horrified by the murder, he made an instant confession to me. Oh, Mr. Holmes, you must save him! We must take counsel how far we can minimize this hideous scandal."

"That can only be done by absolute frankness between us," said Holmes. "You say that Mr. Wilder is not the murderer."

"No, the murderer has escaped."

"Last night," said Sherlock Holmes, smiling, "Mr. Reuben Hayes was arrested at Chesterfield, on my information. I had a telegram from the police this morning."

Said the Duke, staring in amazement at Holmes, "I am right glad to hear it, if it will not react on the fate of James Wilder—my son."

It was Holmes's turn to look astonished.

"This is entirely new to me. I beg you to be more explicit."

"I will conceal nothing," said the Duke. "When I was a very young man I fell deeply in love, but the lady refused to marry me, fearing such a match might mar my career. She died, and left this one child, whom for her sake I have cherished. I could not acknowledge his paternity to the world, but I gave him the best education and have kept him near my person. He surprised my secret, and has presumed ever since on his claim upon me and on his power of provoking a scandal. His presence had something to do with my unhappy marriage. Above all, he hated Arthur, my legitimate heir. I still kept James under my roof because I could see his mother's face in his. But I feared that he should do Arthur a mischief, so I sent Arthur to Dr. Huxtable's school.

"James came into contact with Hayes, because the man was my tenant, and James acted as agent. The fellow was a rascal, but James became intimate with him—he had always a taste for low company. When James determined to kidnap Arthur, he availed himself of the man's service. You remember that I wrote to Arthur on that last day. By making unscrupulous use of his duties as my secretary, James duped the lad into doing what James wanted him to do."

How did James induce young Arthur to leave the school secretly?

Across

1 "More matter, with less ___"
4 Envelop
8 Hindu god of fire
12 What extremes do
14 ___-fire
16 Air pollutant
17 Twining stem
18 Turkish statesman
19 Petruchio's beloved
20 Put in
22 Red-pepper pods
24 Small sofa
25 Between knee and ankle
26 "Take ___ up tenderly"
27 Pawners
31 Fists: Slang
34 Bring about
35 Murmur
36 ___ *Spake Zarathustra*
37 Flounders' family connections

38 Kind of steward
39 *Ben-___*
40 Jesse or Henry
41 Walnut, hickory, etc.
42 River in "Kashmiri Song"
44 Partner of heir
45 Take ___ (travel by motor coach)
46 Made the first bid
49 Award for college athlete
52 ". . . there ___ little cloud . . ."
54 Passageway into a pit
55 Smallest continent, for short
57 You, old style
58 Reputation
59 Up ___ air
60 Hit the ___ (parachute)
61 U. S. citizen
62 Stamping devices
63 These: Fr.

Down

1 Both: Comb. form
2 Homonym of reigns or rains
3 On edge
4 Litterateur
5 Indian princess
6 Legless animal
7 Symbol of neatness
8 Inviting
9 Objective
10 Marginal comment
11 Natives of: Suffix
13 Grows grinders
15 Browning's "My Last ___"
21 Itineraries: Abbr.
23 Play at ___ and seek
25 Swings around
27 Fainter
28 Resound
29 English measure of length
30 ___ up (absorbs)

31 Theological degrees
32 Exclamation meaning "no"
33 Turkish river to the Caspian Sea
34 Stupors
37 Warrior of old Japan
38 ___ *from the Portuguese*
40 Be in agreement
41 Miseries
43 Last mentioned of two
44 Maple-tree spouts
46 "The Lady ___ Tiger?"
47 Moral system
48 Asian wild dog
49 Actress Turner
50 Cheese named for Netherlands town
51 "___, you old gypsy man"
52 Italian wine district
53 Web-footed diving birds
56 ___ so weiter

Puzzle XI:
The Adventure of the Priory School—Part 2

Solution and epilogue on page 152

__ __ __ __ __   __ __ __ __ __   __ __ __ __ , __   __ __ __ __ __ __ __ ,

40 Across 46 Across   31 Across 49 Across

__ __ __ __ __ __ __   __ __ __ __   __ __ __ __

20 Across   10 Down 59 Across

__ __ __ __ __ __ __ ,   __ __ __ __ ,   __ __ __ __ __ __   __ __ __ __ __ __

15 Down   58 Across 8 Down   1 Across 39 Across

__ __ __ __ __   __ __ __ __   __ __ __ __ .

12 Across 40 Across 59 Across 41 Across

The Adventure of the Second Stain

It was on a Tuesday morning in autumn, in a decade which must remain nameless, that Sherlock Holmes and Dr. Watson unexpectedly became hosts to the austere Premier of Britain, Lord Bellinger, and the handsome Right Honorable Trelawney Hope, Secretary for European Affairs. As the notables sat on the settee, it was easy to see from their worn faces that business most pressing had brought them to Baker Street.

"I discovered my loss this morning, Mr. Holmes, and informed Lord Bellinger; we came at his suggestion," said Trelawney Hope.

"Have you informed the police?" asked Holmes.

"No, sir," said the Premier decisively. "To inform the police, is to inform the public. The missing secret document is of such a nature that peace or war may hang on its being recovered."

"Under what circumstances has the document disappeared?"

"The letter—it was from a foreign potentate—was received six days ago," said Trelawney Hope. "I did not trust it to my office safe at night, but brought it each evening to my house in Whitehall Terrace, and kept it in my bedroom locked in a dispatch box. I put it there last night at half-past seven; this morning it was gone. My wife and I will swear that no one could have entered the room after we retired at half-past eleven."

"Then for four hours the box had lain unguarded?"

"My wife went to the theatre, but I was at home all evening. Our servants are trustworthy, and could not have known of the letter."

"Surely your wife knew?"

"No, sir. I said nothing to my wife until I missed the paper this morning. Only members of the Cabinet and two departmental officials know of the letter; I believe no one abroad has seen it."

"Now, sir, I must ask what this letter contains," said Holmes.

"I can say only that the envelope is long and of a blue color."

"If you cannot tell me," said Holmes, "I cannot help you."

The Premier sprang to his feet, then composed himself. "We accept your terms, Mr. Holmes, and rely on your honor and Dr. Watson's. The letter refers angrily to our recent Colonial developments. It is so provocative that its publication could lead to war."

Holmes wrote down a name and handed the paper to the Premier.

"It was he. We have informed him by cipher of the letter's loss. We believe he understands that he acted in a hot-headed manner; it would be the greatest blow to him if it came out."

"Then it is in the interest of his enemies to publish this letter, to make a breach between his country and ours."

Trelawney Hope groaned; the Premier put a kind hand upon him.

"Where in your house is your bedroom located?" asked Holmes.

"It is on the second floor; it has only one entrance."

"Then let us presume that no one could have entered it between half-past seven and half-past eleven but one of your servants. To whom would the thief take the letter? To one of three leading international spies, whose names are known to me. If one has disappeared since last night, we will have some indication as to where the document has gone. I shall make inquiries."

"I believe you are right, Mr. Holmes," said the Premier. "Rather than take it to an Embassy in London, a spy would carry so valuable a prize to headquarters with his own hands."

When the two statesmen had left, Holmes pondered the problem. "If it's on the market, I'll buy it—it's all a question of money. I shall see Oberstein, La Rothiere, and Eduardo Lucas."

Watson, who had been glancing at the morning papers, looked up. "Eduardo Lucas? He was murdered last night," he said.

Holmes snatched the paper from Watson, and read it quickly.

> *Mr. Eduardo Lucas, popular in society circles, was murdered last night at his residence on Godolphin Street. He was a bachelor of thirty-four; his household consisted of Mrs. Pringle, housekeeper, and his valet Mitton. Mrs. Pringle had retired for the night to the top floor; Mitton was visiting a friend. At a quarter to twelve, Police-Constable Barrett, noticing the door of No. 16 ajar, and receiving no answer to his knock, entered the front room. It was in a state of wild disorder. Lucas had been stabbed with a dagger, plucked from one of the walls. There was no robbery.*

"This is no coincidence," said Holmes. "We must find the connection. Fortunately, the police know only of Lucas's murder."

Mrs. Hudson entered, bringing a lady's card on her salver.

"Ask Lady Hilda Trelawney Hope to step up," said Holmes.

The most lovely woman in London, the daughter of the Duke of Belminster, came in, terror shadowing her classic features.

"Has my husband been here, Mr. Holmes?"

"Yes, madam," he said.

"I implore you not to tell him that I came here." Holmes bowed coldly and motioned the lady to a chair. "There is complete confidence between my husband and me—but for politics. I know that a paper has disappeared. I assure you it is best for my husband that I know all. What was this paper?"

"Madam, what you ask is really impossible."

"Will my husband's career suffer through this incident?"

"Unless it is set right, it may have an unfortunate effect."

"Ah!" Lady Hilda sank her face in her hands.

Holmes would divulge no more, and the distressed lady left.

Shortly thereafter, Holmes was off to Godolphin Street. That day and the next two, he returned home in a taciturn and morose mood. The newspapers reported that Lucas's housekeeper and his valet had complete alibis. The dead man's papers had not been tampered with. At times Lucas had visited Paris three months on end, but had always left Mitton at Godolphin Street.

For three mornings the murder remained a mystery, though Holmes informed Watson that Inspector Lestrade had taken him into his confidence in the case. On the fourth day a dispatch from Paris in the *Daily Telegraph* seemed to solve the murder.

> *Mme. Henri Fournaye, returning from a trip to London on Tuesday, was reported to the authorities by her servants as being incoherent and insane. An examination showed that she had developed an incurable mania. Evidence connects her with the murder of Eduardo Lucas, who was killed in London Monday night. Photographs have proved that M. Henri Fournaye and Eduardo Lucas were one and the same. Mme. Fournaye had suffered severe attacks of jealousy; it is conjectured that she killed her husband during such an attack. A woman answering to her description attracted attention at Charing Cross Station on Tuesday morning by erratic behavior.*

"This report," Holmes remarked to Watson, "does not help us in our real task. Where is the letter? Why has it not been published? Did this mad wife carry it off? Ah, a message from the front!" He glanced at the note the page boy had brought up. "Lestrade has observed something of interest. Let us go to Godolphin Street."

At Lucas's house, Holmes and Watson were admitted by an affable constable, and taken to Lestrade in the front room. The violent crime committed there had left an ugly stain on the small rug that lay in the center of the room on the polished wood floor.

"Seen the Paris news?" asked Lestrade. "No doubt it's just as they say. But I want to show you something—the kind of queer thing you take an interest in. After a crime of this sort we are very careful to keep things in position—move nothing. You see that stain on the rug? A great deal of blood must have soaked through—but there is no stain on the floor to correspond!" He lifted a corner of the rug. "See? Now, I'll show you the explanation. There *is* a second stain, but it doesn't correspond with the rug's." As he spoke, he turned over another part of the rug, and there was a great crimson spill on the floor. "Now, Mr. Holmes, who could have moved the rug, and why?"

"Has that constable been in charge of the place all the time?" asked Holmes, trying to suppress his excitement. As Lestrade nodded, he continued, "Question him carefully, but don't do it before us. You're more likely to get a confession out of him alone. Ask how he dared admit people and leave them alone in this room."

"I'll get it out of him!" vowed Lestrade, as he left the room.

"Now, Watson, now!" cried Holmes. They threw back the rug, and Holmes clawed at the squares of wood beneath it. One hinged back; Holmes plunged his hand into the hole—it was empty!

"Quick, Watson, let's get the rug back!" Holmes was leaning against the mantelpiece when Lestrade returned with the constable.

"Tell these gentlemen of your misconduct!" ordered Lestrade.

"He lifted a corner of the rug."

"I meant no harm, sir. The young woman came to the door last evening—wanted to see where the crime was done. When she saw the mark on the rug, she fainted. I couldn't revive her with water, so I went round to the Ivy Plant for brandy. When I returned she was gone—ashamed of herself, I daresay."

"What time was it? Did she come here only once?" asked Holmes.

"Only once, sir. It was just growing dusk."

"Come, Watson, we have work elsewhere. Thank you, Lestrade."

The repentant constable took Holmes and Watson to the door to let them out. Holmes turned on the step and held up something for the constable to see. The constable stared intently.

"Good Lord, sir!" he cried. Holmes put his finger to his lips, to signal the constable to say nothing.

What did Holmes show the constable that so astonished him?

Across

1 Hinged metal fasteners
6 ____-de-sac
9 Fragrance
13 Available, as pub ale
14 Indeed, in Ireland
16 Prevalent
17 Accustom
18 *The ____ Dorian Gray*
20 Calamitous collapse
22 Him, to Hans
23 Bird that mimics human speech
24 Counts calories
26 Expenditure of energy
28 Calf's cry
30 Jeopardy
32 Anaconda
33 Cities in Ohio and Peru
35 Small drum
39 Musical closing
41 Bellini opera

43 Fifth canonical hour
44 Stop talking: Slang
46 Nottingham's river
48 Silver State: Abbr.
49 One of the Montagues
51 "____ America singing . . ."
53 "____ miracle of rare device"
56 The first one was called Eve
58 New Deal agency initials
59 Stevedores' union, for short
61 Small fowl
65 English landscape painter
68 Claw
69 Woman's coiffure
70 Inlets
71 American poet Doolittle
72 ____ out of (expel from)
73 ____ McCoy
74 Inventor Howe

Down

1 Tilled the soil
2 Granddaughter of George VI
3 Counterfoil
4 Show off
5 Sale item
6 Early king of France
7 Swiss canton
8 Places
9 Hockey great
10 ". . . let us ____ make men free"
11 "The days ____ youth . . ."
12 Rig anew
15 Not the same
19 Ailing
21 Admit
25 Killer of Cock Robin
27 Custard tart
28 Lout
29 Luck is one
31 Girl in Salinger story
32 Between a and e

34 Speck of dust
36 ____ fide
37 Lollapalooza
38 Race the motor
40 Invisible emanation
42 Soul
45 Assume as fact
47 ". . . lower ____ angels"
50 Cheekbone
52 Necessitate
53 Bring on oneself
54 Figure of speech
55 Harpsichordist Landowska
57 Corpulent
60 ____ of all right
62 "And ____ ask is a tall ship . . ."
63 Style, in Seville
64 Asian sheep
66 Turf
67 ____-di-dah

Puzzle XII:
The Adventure of the Second Stain

Solution and epilogue on page 153

___ ___ ___ _   _____ ____   ___ _____

53 Across   18 Across   29 Down

_____, _____ _____ ___ ____

71 Across   43 Across   15 Down   47 Down

_____ _____ _____

56 Across   73 Across 65 Across

___ __ __.

21 Down

Intriguing Unpublished Cases

P ". . . I have notes of many hundreds of cases to which I have never alluded," wrote Dr. Watson. But he and Sherlock Holmes did allude to more than seventy intriguing adventures that Watson didn't have the time to publish, or that Holmes wanted withheld for reasons of state or because the world was not yet ready for them.

Many years after Conan Doyle's death, his son, Adrian, decided to write up some of the alluded-to cases. With the collaboration of John Dickson Carr, the mystery writer, eleven of these were cleverly plotted, written in the style of Conan Doyle, and published as *The Exploits of Sherlock Holmes*.

But many delightfully tantalizing cases remain untold. Who has not wished to know more about . . .

● The Dundas separation case, in which the husband was a teetotaler, there was no other woman, and the conduct complained of was that he had drifted into the habit of winding up every meal by taking out his false teeth and hurling them at his wife.

● The repulsive story of the red leech and the terrible death of Crosby, the banker.

● The case involving Mathews, who knocked out Holmes's left canine in the waiting room at Charing Cross.

● The dreadful business of the Albernetty family that was first brought to Holmes's notice by the depth to which the parsley had sunk into the butter on a hot day.

● The case of the inscrutable woman at Margate, whom Holmes suspected because she had no powder on her nose—a clue which proved to be decisive.

● The shocking affair of the Dutch steamship *Friesland*, which so nearly cost Holmes and Watson their lives.

● The tale of the terrible murderer, Bert Stevens, who wanted Holmes to get him cleared, and of whom Holmes had exclaimed, "Was there ever a more mild-mannered, Sunday-school young man?"

● The tracking and arrest of Huret, the Boulevard assassin—an exploit which won for Holmes a handwritten letter of thanks from the French President and the Order of the Legion of Honor.

The Gourmets of Baker Street

*O*Sharing a flat at 221B Baker Street provided a special boon to Sherlock
Holmes and Dr. Watson in the early years of their professional careers
when money was rather scarce. Not only did they live in comfortable
quarters which neither could afford on his own, but they also had the ministra-
tions of Mrs. Hudson, the landlady nonpareil, one of whose duties was to take
care of the "inner man."

Mrs. Hudson kept an abundant larder, she served hot breakfasts and
excellent dinners, and took orders when Holmes or Watson wanted something
special. From the start they dined and wined very well.

In *The Sign of Four*, the second Holmes novel, Holmes invited Athelney
Jones of Scotland Yard to have dinner with him and Watson. "I have oysters
and a brace of grouse, with something a little choice in white wines."

Among the fancier foods mentioned in the Holmes stories were other game
birds, such as woodcock and partridge. Wine usually accompanied dinner:
Chianti, Tokay, Montrachet.

In "The Adventure of the Noble Bachelor," Holmes invited his client, Lord
St. Simon, and two other guests to supper, at which time he intended to
impart disappointing news to the nobleman. To ease the lord's impending
discomfiture, Holmes had ordered up, as Watson put it, "a quite epicurean
little cold supper. . . . There were a couple of brace of cold woodcock, a
pheasant, a *pâté de foie gras* pie with a group of ancient and cobwebby bottles."
Sad to say, on hearing that due to certain complications his American mil-
lionairess bride could no longer be his, Lord St. Simon left without eating his
supper.

Although Sherlock Holmes enjoyed dining well, he could take food or leave
it alone. When he was involved in an absorbing case, he would eat simply, or
he would go without food for long stretches of time.

In "The Five Orange Pips," Holmes had been out all day seeking a clue to
avenge the murder of his client John Openshaw. As Watson related Holmes's
return home, it was "nearly ten o'clock before he entered, looking pale and
worn." He walked to the sideboard, tore a piece from the loaf, and devoured it
voraciously.

"You are hungry," Watson remarked.

"Starving. It had escaped my memory. I have had nothing since breakfast,"
said Holmes.

"Nothing?"

"Not a bite. I had no time to think of it."

What Holmes could not do without was food for thought. "My mind," he
said, "rebels at stagnation. Give me problems, give me work, give me the most
abstruse cryptogram, or the most intricate analysis, and I am in my own
proper atmosphere."

"*The Hound of the Baskervilles.*"

The Hound of the Baskervilles & Puzzles

The Curse of the Baskervilles

D r. Watson, coming down to breakfast one morning in the fall of 1889, found Sherlock Holmes examining a walking stick with a silver band engraved, "To James Mortimer, M.R.C.S., from his friends of the C.C.H., 1884." It had been left the night before by a man who had called while Holmes and Watson were out. Holmes scanned the stick with his lens, then handed it to Watson.

"Well, Watson, what can you say of our unknown visitor?"

"From the looks of this knocked-about stick," said Watson importantly, trying to follow Holmes's methods, "I think Dr. Mortimer is a country practitioner, successful, middle-aged, and well-liked by his friends of the Something Hunt."

"The man is certainly a country practitioner," agreed Holmes. "But it is more likely that the stick was a gift from his friends at Charing Cross Hospital when he left there, obviously to start in practice for himself. He was not successful or middle-aged, or he would have been on the hospital staff, and would not have drifted to the country. He was a house doctor. He is young, unambitious, amiable, absent-minded, and he has a small dog."

"I have no means of checking on your last statements," said Watson, a bit ruffled, "but I can find out about the man's age and career." Taking down his Medical Directory, he read aloud:

> Mortimer, James, M.R.C.S. 1882. Grimpen, Dartmoor, Devon. House surgeon, from 1882 to 1884, at Charing Cross Hospital. Winner of the Jackson prize for Comparative Pathology. Medical Officer for parishes of Grimpen and Thorsely.

"As to my unchecked adjectives," said Holmes with a smile, "it is my experience that it is only an amiable man who receives testimonials, only an unambitious man who abandons London, and only an absent-minded one who loses his stick—which his dog often carries, the teeth marks being plainly visible."

While speaking, Holmes had been pacing the room. Stopping suddenly at the window, he exclaimed, "By Jove, I see the dog on our very doorstep, and there is the ring of its master!"

In a few moments a tall, thin man entered. He wore a dingy frock coat; on his beaklike nose were gold-rimmed glasses. Seeing the stick, he cried joyfully, "I wouldn't lose it for the world! It was given me when I married and set up practice."

Introductions having been made, Holmes waved Dr. Mortimer to a chair, and asked, "On what matter did you call last night?"

"I am an unpractical man, Mr. Holmes," said Mortimer, "faced with a serious problem. I have in my pocket a manuscript."

"I saw it when you entered. I date it about 1730."

Astonished, Dr. Mortimer drew the paper from his breast pocket. "1742, to be exact," he said. "This manuscript was committed to me by Sir Charles Baskerville, who died so tragically five months ago. I was his friend and doctor. He was a sober man, yet he took seriously the family legend this document relates, and was prepared for just such an end as overtook him."

"But I understand it is something modern and practical on which you wish to consult me," said Holmes.

"Most modern, most practical, a pressing matter which must be decided by tomorrow. But the manuscript is connected with the affair. With your permission I will read it to you. It was written by Hugo Baskerville to his sons Rodger and John."

In a high, crackling voice, Dr. Mortimer started to read:

Of the origin of the Hound of the Baskervilles there have been many statements, yet as I come in a direct line from the first Hugo Baskerville, I write down the story with all belief that it occurred as it is here told.

A hundred years ago, our Manor of Baskerville was held by the same Hugo, a most wild and godless man. This Hugo came to desire the daughter of a yeoman who held lands nearby. But the young maiden would ever avoid him, for she feared his evil name. One Michaelmas night, this Hugo, with six of his wicked companions, stole upon the farm and carried off the maiden, her father and brothers being away. Hugo and his companions brought her to Baskerville Hall, put her in an upper chamber, and sat down to a long carouse.

The fearful maiden came down by the ivy that covers the south wall, and ran homeward across the moor, there being three leagues to her father's farm. A little later Hugo went up to carry her food, and found the bird flown. Rushing down to the dining hall, he swore to the company that he would render his soul to the Powers of Evil that very night if he might but overtake the wench. Crying to his grooms to put the hounds upon her, he leaped upon his black mare, and so off full cry in the moonlight over the moor.

The drunken company, awakening to the deed which was like to be done, took horse and started in pursuit. They had gone a mile when they came on a shepherd, shaking with fright. He said that he had seen the maiden, with hounds on her track, and then Hugo Baskerville had passed on his mare, with a mute, horrible hound of hell running behind him. Cursing, the company rode onward, but soon their skins turned cold, for galloping across the moor came the black mare, trailing bridle and empty saddle. On they rode, coming at last upon the hounds whimpering at the head of a deep dip in the moor. In the center of the dip lay the unhappy maid, dead of fear and fatigue. But it was not her body, nor that of Hugo Baskerville lying near her, which horrified the roysterers. Standing over Hugo, plucking at his throat, stood a great, black beast—a gigantic hound. It turned its blazing eyes and dripping jaws upon the company; they fled screaming with terror.

Such is the tale of the hound which has since plagued our family, many of

" 'In the center of the dip lay the unhappy maid.' "

whom have died suddenly, bloodily. Forbear to cross the moor in the dark when the Powers of Evil are exalted.

When Dr. Mortimer had finished reading the narrative, he stared at Sherlock Holmes and asked, "Do you not find it interesting?"

"To a collector of fairy tales," said Holmes, yawning.

"Now, Mr. Holmes, I will read something more recent," said Mortimer, drawing from his pocket a folded newspaper. "This is the *Devon County Chronicle* of May 14th." He read aloud:

The sudden death of Sir Charles Baskerville has saddened the country. Though he had resided here only a short time, he had won the affection and respect of all who knew him. Having made his fortune in South Africa, Sir Charles had returned to Baskerville Hall two years ago. He was a generous and charitable man, as being a childless widower, his desire was to benefit the entire countryside. He lived simply; his only indoor servants were a married couple named Barrymore.

While the inquest did not entirely clear up the circumstances of Sir Charles's death, foul play is not suspected. He had suffered from heart disease and acute depression, as Dr. James Mortimer, his friend and physician, has attested.

The facts in the case are simple. Sir Charles was in the habit every night of walking down the yew alley of Baskerville Hall. On May 4th he informed Barrymore that he was going to London the next day. That night he went for his customary walk, during which he usually smoked a cigar. When he did not return, Barrymore went in search of him. The day had been wet, so Sir Charles's footprints were easily traced. Halfway down the walk is a gate leading on to the moor. There were indications that Sir Charles had stood for a little time there. He then proceeded down the alley. His body was found at the far end. An unexplained fact is Barrymore's report that the footprints changed after Sir Charles passed the gate; from then on he appeared to be walking on his toes. His face showed great distortion, but this is a symptom in death from cardiac exhaustion; the post-mortem showed chronic organic disease.

The coroner's finding has put an end to the romantic stories about the case. Inquiries are being made to locate the next of kin, Mr. Henry Baskerville, son of Sir Charles's younger brother, who went last heard of was farming in America.

"These are the public facts in the case," said Mortimer.

"Then let me have the private ones," said Holmes.

"As a man of science, I did not want to endorse a popular superstition, or increase Baskerville Hall's grim reputation, so I withheld information I will now reveal to you, Mr. Holmes.

"The moor is sparsely inhabited. Except for Mr. Frankland of Lafter Hall, and Mr. Stapleton, the naturalist, Sir Charles was the only one I spent much time with. Recently it became plain to me that his nervous system was at the breaking point. He had taken the legend of the hound to heart—he feared a dreadful fate, would not go out on the moor at night. Several times he had asked me, with great excitement, if I had heard the baying of a hound, or had seen any strange creature. It was at my advice that he was about to go to London; I thought that a few months in town would distract him. Mr. Stapleton, a mutual friend, was of the same opinion. On the night of Sir Charles's death, Barrymore sent Perkins the groom to fetch me. I carefully examined the yew alley and Sir Charles's body. I was able to corroborate all the facts mentioned at the inquest. But one false statement had been made by Barrymore. He said there were no traces on the ground round the body. He did not observe any. But I did—a little distance off, fresh and clear footprints."

"A man's or a woman's?" asked Holmes.

What was Dr. Mortimer's answer? A man's or a woman's footprints?

Across

1 Bees' storehouse
5 Author of *Gulliver's Travels*
10 ___ dansant (tea dance)
13 Ben Adhem
14 Vietnamese capital
15 Ship's frame
17 Dweller in a cold climate
19 Auspices
20 ___ off (rile)
21 Dobbin's dinner
22 Hemingway
24 It may be grand or petty
25 Smart one
26 "But ___ work is never done"
29 Souvenir
33 Upright
34 Kind of band
36 Play it by ___
37 Urgent
38 College administrators

39 Dog in *Peter Pan*
40 Bank-depositor's funds: Abbr.
41 Salvers
42 Begin to occur
43 Nor yet
45 "___ a tangled web . . ."
46 Ginger plants
47 "What's ___ for me?"
48 Belgian seaport
51 Autocrat
52 Promissory note
55 Business company
56 "___ on the sands of time"
59 Exchange fee
60 Soft-palate lobe
61 Lily plant
62 "___ any drop to drink"
63 Subsequently
64 Caustics

Down

1 *You___ Go Home Again*
2 Bassoon's brother
3 Additional
4 Excepting
5 Fleeces
6 Like a toad's skin
7 Tabard, and others
8 Antagonist
9 Indefatigable
10 On that account
11 Mammoth
12 Ancient Olympics country
16 Nav. landing vessel
18 Autograph collector: Slang
23 Dreamer's ocular actions
24 Ms. Austen
25 ". . . ___ house is his castle"
26 Chief Teutonic god
27 In the bag
28 Thanks, in Toulon
30 Below: Poet.

31 Russian girl's name
32 Praying figure
34 ___ up (takes it)
35 Skate
38 "The City of ___ Night"
39 Eft
41 Now and ___
42 Bake eggs
44 Quiver
45 Equal
47 Cordage fiber
48 ___ piece (alike)
49 Aries or Aquarius
50 Chamber-music group
51 Race-track tipster
52 Under the surface
53 Sioux
54 ___ up (exhausts)
57 Eggs
58 Like: Suffix

Puzzle XIII: *The Curse of the Baskervilles*

1	2	3	4		5	6	7	8	9		10	11	12	
13					14						15			16
17			18								19			
20				21					22	23				
			24					25						
26	27	28						29				30	31	32
33					34	35					36			
37				38						39				
40				41					42					
43			44					45						
			46				47							
48	49	50				51					52	53	54	
55				56	57				58					
59				60					61					
	62			63					64					

Solution on page 156

"__ __ __ __ __ __ __ __ __ __ __'__ __ __ __ __
43 Across   25 Down   62 Across

__ __ __ __ __ __ __'__, __ __ __ __ __ __ __ __ __ __ __ __,
26 Across   4 Down 10 Across 37 Across

__ __ __ __ __ __ __ __ __ __ __ __ __ __ __ __ __ __
38 Down   56 Across

__ __ __ __ __ __ __ __ __ __ __ __ __ __ __ __."
48 Down 11 Down 18 Down

The Problem

S herlock Holmes leaned forward, greatly interested.

"You saw the hound's footprints, Dr. Mortimer, yet you said nothing? How was it that no one else remarked on them?"

"The marks were twenty yards from the body—the hound had not approached Sir Charles," said Mortimer. "I, too, would not have thought anything of the marks had I not known of the legend."

"What sort of night was it when Sir Charles died?"

"Damp and raw—if only his poor health had kept him indoors!"

"What is the alley like?"

"Some distance behind the Hall are two lines of old yew hedge, twelve feet high; halfway down, one line is penetrated by the gate to the moor. The walk is eight feet across; between the walk and the hedge lies a strip of grass on either side. There is an exit through a summer house at the far end of the alley."

"Was the moor gate closed?"

"It was closed and padlocked."

"How high is it?"

"About four feet high."

"Then anyone could have got over it. Were there any marks near the gate?"

"None in particular, but Sir Charles had evidently stood there for five or ten minutes—the ash had twice dropped from his cigar."

"No marks found but his own?" asked Holmes. "I should have been there! Why did you not call me in, Dr. Mortimer?"

"I did not wish to make public the facts I have given you, Mr. Holmes. Besides, there is a realm in which the most acute detective is helpless. Since the tragedy, I have heard of several incidents bordering on the supernatural that occurred before Sir Charles died. Three hard-headed countrymen have seen on the moor a creature like the hound—huge, luminous, ghastly, spectral."

"If you hold this view, why have you come to see me?"

"As a trustee and executor of Sir Charles's will, I need advice as to what I should do with Sir Henry Baskerville of Canada, who arrives in an hour. He is Sir Charles's sole heir. Sir Charles was the eldest of three brothers. The middle brother, who died young, was the father of this lad Henry. The third brother, Rodger, was the black sheep of the family; he fled from England to Central America, where he died in 1876, unmarried. Henry is the last of the Baskervilles. What would you advise me to do with him?"

"Why should he not go to the home of his fathers?"

"It seems as though every Baskerville meets an evil fate there. From all accounts Sir Henry is an excellent fellow; I feel that Sir Charles would have warned me against bringing him to the Hall. Yet the prosperity of the countryside depends on his presence; if the Hall is untenanted, Sir Charles's good work will crash down."

"If your supernatural theory is correct," said Holmes, "it could do the young man evil in London as easily as in Devonshire. I recommend that you take a cab, and proceed to Waterloo to meet Sir Henry. And then say nothing to him at all until I see you both tomorrow morning. I shall be obliged if you and Sir Henry will call here at ten. One more question, Dr. Mortimer. You say that before Sir Charles's death three people saw the apparition upon the moor. Did any see it after? None? Ah, thank you."

After Dr. Mortimer left, Watson prepared to go out.

"I shall spend the day thinking about Dr. Mortimer's problem," said Holmes. "We shall compare impressions this evening."

Watson knew that solitude was necessary to Holmes's hours of intense concentration during which he weighed the evidence, and constructed alternative theories. The doctor spent the day at his club, and returned at nine to the smoke-filled sitting room.

"Guess where I've been," said Holmes. "I've been to Devonshire—in spirit. I sent down for the ordnance map of the Baskerville Hall portion of the moor." He unrolled a large map on the table. "This is Baskerville Hall in the middle."

"With a wood round it?" asked Watson.

"Exactly. The yew alley must stretch along this line, with the moor on the right of it. Here is Dr. Mortimer's hamlet of Grimpen. Within a five-mile radius of the Hall are only a few dwellings—here is Lafter Hall, Mr. Frankland's residence, and there is the house which may be the home of Stapleton, the naturalist. And here are two farmland houses, High Tor and Foulmire. Fourteen miles away is the great convict prison of Princetown. Between and around these points is the desolate, lifeless moor." Holmes paused. "And now two questions await us. One is whether any crime has been committed; the second is, what is the crime and how was it committed? Have you thought about the case?"

"It is very bewildering," said Watson.

"There are certain points of distinction about it. The change in Sir Charles's footprints—what do you make of that?"

"Mortimer said the man had walked on tiptoe part of the way."

"He only repeated what some fool had said at the inquest. Why should a man walk on tiptoe down the alley? He was running, Watson, running desperately, running for his life, until he burst his heart and fell dead."

"Running from what?" asked Watson.

"There lies our problem. He was crazed with fears that came to him across the moor before he began to run. Only a man who had lost his wits would have run *from* the house instead of towards it. Then, again, whom was he waiting for that night, and why was he waiting in the yew alley?"

"Why do you think he was waiting for someone?"

Besides the cigar ash, what other clue made Holmes certain that Sir Charles had waited for someone at the moor gate?

Across

1 Waterway between two seas
7 Dear, in Deauville
13 River in Massachusetts
15 Kind of game
16 Merrymaking
17 Pungent detergent
18 Devoured
19 Scourge
21 Traipse
22 Pitti, for one
25 Wolfe, and others
28 Baronet's title
29 Skulls
33 It "hath a thousand eyes"
36 _____ Baba
37 Prohibition
38 Skagerrak seaport
39 The big house

40 "Love _____ leave me"
41 Western lariat
43 U. S. P. S. chief
44 _____ Haute
45 Federal health program
47 Cattle genus
48 Hebrew month
49 Anointed
53 Black bird
56 Quoter
58 Consisting of one only: Comb. form
59 Tranquilizes
62 Anticipated with fear
65 Soda cracker
66 E. H. _____, U. S. actor
67 _____ try (Knock oneself out)
68 "He _____ of an age . . ."

Down

1 Hassle
2 Between eta and iota
3 Untwist
4 "But where _____ the snows . . ."
5 On the sick list
6 Less wordy
7 Snapshotter's device
8 Homonym of hymn
9 WWII area
10 Tree-trunk's annual growth
11 Porpoise genus
12 Old-fashioned oath
14 Orchestral comp.
15 Hosing down
20 Raw, as weather
23 _____ the dark (blind guess)
24 Townsman
26 Canadian prov.
27 Blue-eyed cat
30 Over: Ger.
31 Anchor

32 Resentful
33 Group standard
34 "Is this a dagger which _____. . ."
35 Word before eye or hand
36 Evaluate
42 Acid group: Comb. form
44 Place-name ending
46 Go up
47 Alaska's Point _____
50 Famous cough-drop name
51 January, in Jerez
52 "I _____ Know What Time It Was"
53 Helper, for short
54 Stingy
55 To no purpose
57 They revise mss.
60 _____ disadvantage
61 Chemical element Sn
63 Age: It.
64 All-purpose exclamations

Puzzle XIV: *The Problem*

1	2	3	4	5	6			7	8	9	10	11	12
13					14		15						
16							17						
18				19		20					21		
22		23	24			25			26	27			
		28				29					30	31	32
33	34	35			36				37				
38					39					40			
41			42		43			44					
45				46			47						
		48					49			50	51	52	
53	54	55		56		57			58				
59		60	61			62		63	64				
65						66							
67							68						

Solution on page 156

_____ _____, _____, _____
28 Across 13 Across   5 Down   33 Across

_____, ____ ____ _____
20 Down   68 Across   15 Across

_____ _____ _____ _____.
55 Down   54 Down   62 Across   31 Down

Three Broken Threads

Promptly at ten the next morning Dr. Mortimer and Sir Henry arrived at Baker Street. The baronet was a small, alert, dark-eyed man of thirty, sturdily built, with a strong, weather-beaten face that bespoke an outdoor life. He was clad in ruddy tweeds.

"If Dr. Mortimer had not proposed coming here, Mr. Holmes," said Sir Henry, "I should have come on my own. I understand you think out puzzles, and I received a strange one this morning."

He laid on the table an envelope addressed in rough letters to "Sir Henry Baskerville, Northumberland Hotel." It was postmarked "Charing Cross," and dated the preceding evening.

"No one could have known I was going to that hotel. It was decided on when I met Dr. Mortimer. He has been staying with friends."

Holmes took out of the envelope a paper containing a single sentence, made up of cut-out printed words pasted on it. It read:

As you value your life or reason keep away from the moor.

"Nothing supernatural about this, Dr. Mortimer," said Holmes.

"The sender may think the business supernatural," said Mortimer.

"What business?" asked Sir Henry sharply.

"You shall know all before you leave this room, Sir Henry," promised Holmes. "Have you yesterday's *Times*, Watson?"

Holmes quickly ran his eyes up and down the columns of the newspaper. "Here it is!" he exclaimed, and read aloud a paragraph which had, scattered through it, the pasted words.

"Remarkable!" said Mortimer. "You knew the very paper and the day!"

"Knowledge of types is elementary to the crime expert. That of a *Times* leading article is quite distinctive. As the message was sent yesterday, it was at yesterday's paper I looked first."

"Have you read anything else in the message?"

"The characters on the envelope are rough, but *The Times* is read by educated people. Probably the writer wanted to conceal his own fluent handwriting. The words are not gummed on in an accurate line—pointing to carelessness or to agitation and hurry. I should guess the latter. The address was written in a hotel—both the pen and ink have given the writer trouble. Halloa! What's this?" He held the message an inch or two from his eyes. "It's nothing—not even a watermark on this paper. Well, Sir Henry, anything else to report?"

"I have lost one of my boots," said the baronet, smiling. "I put them both outside my door last night, and there was only one in the morning. The chap who cleans them knew nothing about it, and the worst of it is—I have never had them on. They were new tan boots, and I wanted them varnished."

"As no one can use the boot, it will be returned," said Holmes.

"And now, Mr. Holmes," said Sir Henry with decision, "it is time you kept your promise. What is this supernatural business?"

"Dr. Mortimer," said Holmes, "please tell your story."

The baronet listened with deep attention, and said, when Mortimer had completed his tale, "I have heard of the hound ever since I was in the nursery. Now there's this affair of the letter."

"It is a kind message, warning you of danger," said Holmes.

"Or it may be meant to scare me away."

"We have to make a practical decision, Sir Henry," said Holmes, "as to whether it is advisable for you to go to the Hall."

"There is no devil in hell, Mr. Holmes, and no man on earth who can prevent me from going to the home of my own people. I mean to continue the good work started by my uncle Charles. Meanwhile, I should like to have a quiet hour by myself at my hotel. Suppose you and Dr. Watson come round and have lunch with us at two."

Holmes and Watson accepted the invitation. Sir Henry did not want a cab called for him and Mortimer, saying he wished to walk.

As soon as the door closed behind their visitors, Holmes cried, "Your hat and boots, Watson, quick! Not a moment to lose!" They hurried down into the street, and started to follow Sir Henry and Mortimer. On Regent Street Sir Henry stopped to look into a shop window. Holmes did the same, and an instant later he uttered a cry—he had seen a hansom cab on the other side of the street with a black-bearded man inside. It had halted when Sir Henry had halted, and then proceeded slowly again when the baronet started walking.

"That's our man, Watson!" cried Holmes. "Come along!"

But the man, seeing them, shouted to his driver, and the cab flew madly off. Holmes looked round wildly for another—in vain.

"There now!" he said bitterly. "Was ever such bad luck and bad management, too. On observing the cab I should instantly have walked in the other direction, and have hired a cab there."

"What a pity we did not get the cab's number," said Watson.

"My dear Watson, clumsy as I have been, I did get the number. No. 2704 is our man. Well, there is no object in following our friends now; it was their shadow I was looking for, and he is gone. I knew Sir Henry was being followed—else how was his hotel so quickly known?"

Walking on, Holmes and Watson stepped into a messenger office, where Holmes hired his young friend Cartwright to search the wastepaper of twenty-three hotels in the Charing Cross area for a cut-out page of *The Times*. Giving the boy a copy of the page, Holmes instructed him to wire a report to Baker Street before evening.

"And now, Watson, we shall wire for the identity of No. 2704."

Arriving at two at the Northumberland for lunch, Holmes asked the clerk if he might look at the register. Two names had been added after Baskerville's.

"Holmes hired his young friend Cartwright."

Pretending that he knew the newcomers, Holmes learned from the clerk that they were old, frequent guests.

"Now we know, Watson," said Holmes, "that the people who are interested in Sir Henry are not at this hotel—anxious as they are to watch him, they do not want to be seen by him."

Going up to Sir Henry's floor, they were surprised to find him in the hall, flushed with anger, an old dusty boot in his hand.

"They've gone too far this time, Mr. Holmes!" he cried. "If that chap can't find my missing boot there will be trouble. First it was my new tan boot, and now it's an old black one!" An elderly waiter appeared on the scene. "Have you got it. Speak out, man!"

"No, sir. But it shall be found—have a little patience."

"What do you make of this, Mr. Holmes?" asked Sir Henry, when the agitated waiter had left. "You look very serious over it!"

"I don't understand it yet. Your case if very complex. We hold several threads; one of them will lead us to the truth."

After a pleasant luncheon, Holmes remarked, "Your decision to go to Baskerville Hall is a wise one, Sir Henry. It will be easier in the country to track down these people who are so interested in you. Do you know you were followed from my house this morning?"

Dr. Mortimer started violently. "Followed! By whom?"

"By a man with a square black beard. Is there any such at Dartmoor?"

"Why, yes. Barrymore, the butler, who is in charge of the Hall."

"We must ascertain if he is really there. May I have two telegraph forms? One will go to Barrymore asking if all is in readiness for Sir Henry; the other to the Grimpen postmaster, requesting that Barrymore's wire be delivered into his own hand, or returned."

"Who is this Barrymore, Dr. Mortimer?" asked Sir Henry.

"The son of the old caretaker, who is dead. He and his wife are a respectable couple. Sir Charles left them £500 each."

"Ha!" said Holmes. "Did they know they would receive this?"

"Yes, Sir Charles often talked of his will. I was left £1000. After all other bequests, the residue of £750,000 went to Sir Henry. The total value of the estate is about a million."

"Dear me! Those are high stakes," said Holmes. "If anything happened to Sir Henry—forgive the hypothesis—who would inherit?"

"A distant cousin, James Desmond, who is an elderly clergyman in Westmoreland. He would be heir to the estate because it is entailed. But Sir Henry may leave his money to whom he chooses."

"And have you made your will, Sir Henry?" asked Holmes.

"Not yet, but house, land, and dollars should go together."

"You must not go to Devonshire alone, Sir Henry. Dr. Mortimer lives too far away from you, and I am too busy. If Dr. Watson would undertake it, there is no better man to have at your side."

Before Watson could reply, Sir Henry had wrung his hand in gratitude. Lured by adventure and complimented by Holmes's words, Watson agreed to go, and plans were made to leave the coming Saturday.

Holmes and Watson had risen to depart, when Sir Henry suddenly dove under a cabinet and triumphantly drew out a tan boot.

"It was not there before lunch," said Dr. Mortimer, mystified.

The waiter was sent for, but said he knew nothing of the matter.

On their return to Baker Street, Holmes and Watson found two telegrams waiting. The postmaster's stated, "Have heard that Barrymore is at the Hall." Cartwright's said, "Cut-out *Times* not found."

"There go two of my threads, Watson."

The doorbell rang, the door opened, and a rough-looking fellow, No. 2704 in person, entered the sitting room. He appeared to be angry.

"I came to ask you to your face what you have against me!"

"Not a thing," Holmes assured him. "I have half a sovereign for you if you can tell me about the fare who watched this house at ten this morning, then followed two gentlemen down Regent Street."

"Seems you know as much as I do already," said the cabman.

"Did he tell you anything about himself?" asked Holmes.

What was the cabman's answer? It broke Holmes's third thread.

Across

1 Energy
4 Aforementioned
8 Canal part
12 River in Italy
13 Anglo-Saxon laborer
14 "_____ eyes are blue as skies"
16 Operative
18 Unit of the Union
19 Burrowing rodent
20 October birthstone
22 Fabulous bird
23 Diamonds: Slang
24 _____ soit qui mal y pense
26 "_____ man, take him for all in all"
28 _____ with the goods
30 Highest: Comb. form
32 Frigga's spouse
33 Belgian river
34 Jan van der _____
35 Musical sign
36 Le Moko of the Casbah
38 Baby foods
40 Persian tiger
43 Daffy
45 Drill-sergeant's shouts
48 Aureole
49 Flying saucers
50 Fifth largest planet
52 Expunges
54 Kind of lamp
56 Lyric-writer Gershwin
57 Highways: Abbr.
58 African lake
60 Author of *The Autocrat of the Breakfast Table*
62 Floral leaf
64 Gentleman's _____
66 U. S. writer Loos
67 New Dehli nurse
68 Verne's submarine captain
69 Shoo!
70 Dirk
71 _____ run (rehearsal)

Down

1 Moralizing
2 Main courses
3 Words by Wordsworth
4 Fist fight
5 "_____ was going up the stair"
6 Bill
7 Abstruse
8 Strong cotton thread
9 "_____ I had heard of Lucy Gray"
10 Pantomime riddle
11 Cattle disease
12 Own up
15 Eat one's words publicly
17 Stick together
21 Now: Sp.
25 In the _____ (for)
27 "No _____ husband than the best of men"
29 Fine proofs
31 Tranquility
37 Luxurious
39 Carbolic acid component
40 Tenzing Norkay, for one
41 Toughens
42 Springy
44 Declare unfit for use
46 More prudish
47 Flowing
51 _____ use for (dislikes)
53 Brilliance
55 "_____ old swimmin' hole!"
59 Moslem titles of respect
61 Advance
63 _____ loss
65 Scottish no

Puzzle XV: *Three Broken Threads*

Solution on page 157

"——— , ——— ——————————— ————
55 Down   64 Across   4 Across

—— ——— —— ———————————— ,
26 Across   16 Across

————— ——— ——————— ——————."
25 Down   40 Across   8 Across   60 Across

The Stapletons of Merripit House

A touch, Watson, an undeniable touch," said Sherlock Holmes, when the cabman told of his bearded fare identifying himself as Sherlock Holmes. The cabman had taken him from Regent Street to Waterloo Station; he was "a toff, about forty, of a middle height."

On Saturday morning, accompanying Watson in his cab to Paddington, Holmes remarked that inquiries he had made concerning James Desmond proved that the elderly clergyman was not involved in the case. Asking Watson for full reports, Holmes gave him a "list."

"Our suspects," said Holmes, "are the Barrymore couple, Perkins, groom at the Hall, two moorland farmers, Dr. Mortimer and his wife, of whom we know nothing. Then there are the naturalist, Stapleton, and his sister, who is said to be beautiful, and Mr. Frankland of Lafter Hall, also an unknown factor, and a neighbor or two. This is an ugly, dangerous business, Watson. Keep your revolver near you night and day, and never relax your precautions."

Sir Henry and Dr. Mortimer had already secured a first-class carriage, and were waiting for Watson on the platform.

"We are sure," said Mortimer in reply to Holmes's first question, "that we were not followed these past two days. We went out together all the time except yesterday afternoon, when we went separate ways."

"That was imprudent," said Holmes gravely. "I beg you, Sir Henry, not to go out alone. Did you get your other boot?"

"No, sir, it is gone forever."

"Interesting," said Holmes. "Well, goodbye, and as the legend says, avoid the moor 'when the powers of evil are exalted.' "

The journey was a swift and pleasant one for Watson and his companions. Young Baskerville was delighted when the train passed through Devon.

"I left here when I was in my teens," he said. "I have never seen the Hall; I lived with my father in a cottage on the South Coast, and from there went to America. I am keen to see the moor."

"There is your first sight of it," said Dr. Mortimer.

Over the green fields and a curve of woods there rose in the distance a low, gray, melancholy hill with a strange jagged summit, dim and vague, like some fantastic landscape in a dream.

The train pulled up at a wayside station, and the young heir and his companions descended to find Perkins waiting with a wagonette. Their coming was evidently a great event, for stationmaster and porters clustered round. Watson was surprised to note at the gate two soldiers with rifles eyeing them closely as they passed.

The carriage had flown down a broad highway, and had turned into a side road, when Dr. Mortimer cried, "Halloa! what is this?" On a steep curve of land was an armed, mounted soldier.

"There's a convict escaped from Princetown, sir," said the groom. "He's been out on the moor three days, but they've had no sight of him yet. It's Selden, the Notting Hill murderer."

Watson remembered the case because of the ferocity of the crime. The brutal murderer's sentence had been commuted due to doubts about his sanity. And now, somewhere in the desolate moor, the fiend was lurking.

The carriage passed through land that grew bleaker and wilder, until it reached the wrought-iron gates of Baskerville Hall. The gateway led into a long, somber drive, at the end of which, in an expanse of turf, stood ancient Baskerville Hall. The center was a heavy block of building, draped in ivy, from which rose crenellated twin towers. To the right and left of the turrets were more modern wings of black granite.

"Welcome, Sir Henry, to Baskerville Hall!" Barrymore had stepped from the shadows to open the door of the wagonette. His wife emerged from the house to help him hand down the bags.

After bidding goodbye to Dr. Mortimer, Sir Henry and Watson walked into the lofty, oak-raftered hall, in which a log fire crackled in the great old-fashioned fireplace. They gazed round at the high windows of old stained glass, the oak panelling, and the stags' heads and coats of arms upon the walls.

"My people's home for five hundred years," said Sir Henry.

Having brought the luggage up, Barrymore returned to the hall. He was a tall, pale, handsome man, with a square black beard.

"Dinner will be ready soon, Sir Henry," he said. "My wife and I will be happy to stay with you until you make new arrangements."

"I hope you do not mean that your wife and you wish to leave."

"Sir Charles's death has made these surroundings very painful to us. His generosity has given us the means to establish ourselves in business. And now, sir, may I show you to your rooms?"

A wide stair led up to the bedrooms in one of the modern wings—Watson's was almost next door to Sir Henry's. Coming down to dinner, they found the dining room, which opened out from the hall, to be a place of gloom and shadow. A dim line of ancestors, in every dress, from Elizabethan to Regency, stared down from the walls.

After dinner, Watson and Sir Henry retired early. From his window, Watson could see beyond the wind-tossed trees a broken fringe of rocks, and the long, low curve of the melancholy moor. Then, suddenly, as he lay wakeful, came the unmistakable sound of a woman sobbing uncontrollably.

The fresh beauty of the following morning dispelled somewhat the grim first impression of Baskerville Hall. At breakfast, Sir Henry commented on the changed atmosphere, but Watson was still troubled by the sounds he had heard in the night.

"Did you hear a woman sobbing last night, Sir Henry?"

"Curious—I did hear something of the sort, but I thought it was a dream. We must ask about this right away." He rang for Barrymore, and asked him if he could account for the sounds.

"There are only two women here," said Barrymore. "The scullery maid, who sleeps in the other wing, and my wife. I can answer for it that the sounds did not come from my wife."

In the corridor, Watson met Mrs. Barrymore, a large, impassive woman. Her eyes were red and the lids swollen—Barrymore had lied.

Knowing Sir Henry would be occupied with matters at the Hall, Watson decided to walk to Grimpen to learn from the postmaster if the telegram had really been placed in Barrymore's own hands.

It was a pleasant walk of four miles along the edge of the moor. The postmaster clearly recalled the telegram.

"My boy here delivered it to Mr. Barrymore—did you not, James?"

"He was up in the loft, so I gave it to Mrs. Barrymore."

"Did you see Mr. Barrymore in the loft?" asked Watson.

When the boy said he had not, the postmaster broke in testily, "If there was a mistake, it is for Mr. Barrymore to complain!"

As Watson walked back along the lonely road, it was plain to him that in spite of Holmes's ruse there was no proof that Barrymore had not been in London all the time. Suddenly his thoughts were interrupted by a voice calling him by name. He turned, expecting to see Dr. Mortimer, but saw instead a stranger. The man was small, slim, cleanshaven, about thirty-five; he wore a straw hat on his flaxen hair, and carried a butterfly net in his hand.

"Excuse me, Dr. Watson," said the man, "but as you passed Dr. Mortimer's surgery, he pointed you out to me. I am Stapleton, of Merripit House. We are all pleased that Sir Henry has come here, and trust he has no superstitious fears of his family's legend."

"I do not think that it is likely," said Watson.

"I was very fond of Sir Charles. Dr. Mortimer had told me of his diseased heart; I feared that the sight of any dog might frighten him to death. Has Mr. Holmes any thoughts on the matter?"

Watson could not hide his surprise at Stapleton's mention of Holmes.

"You could not celebrate Mr. Holmes without being known yourself, Dr. Watson. If you are here, Mr. Holmes is interested in the case. Is he planning to come here? I may be of aid to him and to you."

"He is far too busy," said Watson. "I am here simply to visit my friend, Sir Henry, and I assure you that I need no help of any kind."

"A walk along this path brings us to Merripit House," said Stapleton. "Will you spare an hour to meet my sister?"

Mindful of Holmes's "list," Watson accepted the invitation.

"The moor is a wonderful place," said Stapleton, as they walked along. "Vast, barren, mysterious. I've been here only two years, but I have explored every part. Few men know it better than I do. Do you observe anything remarkable about the plain to the north?"

"It would be a rare place for a gallop," said Watson.

Stapleton laughed. "See those green spots scattered over it? That is the great Grimpen Mire. A false step yonder means death in the quagmire. Yet I can find my way to its heart and return alive."

"But why should you wish to go into so horrible a place?"

"You see the hills beyond? That is where the rare plants and butterflies are, if you have the wit to reach them."

"I shall try my luck some day," said Watson.

"Put such ideas out of your head!" cried Stapleton. "It is only by remembering complex landmarks that I am able to find my way."

A long, low moan, indescribably sad, swept over the moor.

"The peasants say it is the Hound of the Baskervilles," said Stapleton. "But it's mud settling, or some such thing. Or it may be a bittern booming. Yes, the moor is an uncanny place. Look at the hillside yonder, and the stone rings upon it. They are the homes of prehistoric man. You can even see his hearth and couch if you go inside. Oh, excuse me. It is surely Cyclopides."

And off Stapleton went, after the butterfly. As Watson stood watching his eager pursuit, he heard footsteps, and turning round found a woman near him on the path. She had come from the direction of Merripit House. He knew at once from her striking dark beauty that she was Miss Stapleton. He raised his hat and was about to speak, when she cried earnestly, "For God's sake, go straight back to London, and never set foot on the moor again!"

Can you guess why Miss Stapleton warned Watson to leave?

"She cried earnestly, 'For God's sake, go straight back to London!'"

Across

1 Nonprofessional
4 Troop camps
9 ___ signal
13 "Oh, ___ in England . . ."
14 Up the ante
15 East, to Eduardo
16 Olive genus
17 Gumbos
18 Imparted
19 Alexander Graham Bell's assistant
21 White water
23 Mann or Wolfe: Abbr.
25 Pintail duck
26 "___ lions roar . . ."
30 Grudged
34 Latin king
35 Catch in a trap
37 Concise
38 Wife of Geraint
40 ___ long yarn (speak at length)

42 Palm fruit
43 City on the Rhone
45 ___ nous
47 Spread for drying, as grass
48 Staining
50 Pioneers
52 Needlefishes
54 Kind of paper
55 Exclamation of exasperation
57 "___ so many children . . ."
61 Heroine of La Bohéme
62 French impressionist
65 "If wishes ___ horses . . ."
66 Verve
67 Eat into
68 Intentions
69 Pungency
70 Namesakes of Adam's third son
71 They consist of mos.

Down

1 "Whatever ___ Wants"
2 Back up
3 Frothy
4 We, she, etc.
5 ___-leaf cluster
6 Winston Churchill's title
7 Absolute rulers
8 Flavoring seed
9 Credited
10 Secondhand
11 R. R. deps.
12 ". . . the end is not ___"
13 Coarse flax
20 Exclamations of triumph
22 Five: Comb. form
24 Taper a timber
26 "Don't ___ on me"
27 Kissinger
28 Banish
29 Copies the Cheshire-Cat

31 Incensed
32 Organic compound
33 "Little ___ of kindness"
36 "All hope abandon, ye who ___"
39 Condescending
41 Professional performers
44 Unexpected obstacle
46 Engrave
49 Dirties
51 Elbowroom
53 Goggle
55 Seed scars
56 "What a piece of work is ___!"
58 Legatee
59 Heraldic insignia
60 ___ Moines
61 N. Y. C. opera house
63 To no degree
64 Old English letter

Puzzle XVI:
The Stapletons of Merripit House

Solution on page 157

___ ___ ___   ___ ___ ___   ___ ___ ___   ___ ___ ___   ___ ___ ___
57 Across   63 Down 12 Down 61 Down 6 Down

___ ___ ___ ___ ___ ; ___ ___ ___ ___ ___ ___ ___ ___ ___ ___ ___ ___
27 Down   9 Down   19 Across

___ ___   ___ ___   ___ ___ ___   ___ ___ ___   ___ ___ ___ ___ .
13 Across   26 Across   58 Down

103

Report of Dr. Watson

W
hy should I go back?" asked the astonished Watson.

"Man, man!" cried Miss Stapleton, "get away from here at all costs! Hush, my brother is coming. Not a word of what I have said."

"Hello, Beryl," said Stapleton, looking from her to Watson in an unfriendly way. "You have introduced yourselves, I see."

"Yes, I was telling Sir Henry about the beauties of the moor."

"No, no," said Watson. "I am Sir Henry's friend, Dr. Watson."

Miss Stapleton flushed with vexation, but recovering quickly she said, "You will come on, Dr. Watson, and see Merripit House?"

The Stapleton residence was an old moorland house, surrounded by a stunted orchard; the whole place seemed mean and melancholy to Watson. He was surprised, however, when a wizened manservant admitted them to rooms that were large and elegantly furnished.

"Queer spot," said Stapleton, "but we are happy here, are we not, Beryl?" She nodded without conviction. "I had a school in the north, but three of the boys died in an epidemic, and my capital was irretrievably lost. My sister and I are devoted to nature, and the moor offers unlimited study. We have our books, and interesting neighbors. Do you think I might call on Sir Henry this afternoon?"

"I am sure he would be delighted," said Watson.

The Stapletons invited Watson to stay for lunch, but he was eager to get back to his charge, and set off for the Hall. Miss Stapleton surprised him again, this time by appearing before him on the road. She asked him to forget her words of warning.

"But I can't forget," said Watson. "Your words were meant for Sir Henry. Please, please, be frank with me, Miss Stapleton."

"My brother and I were shocked by Sir Charles's death," she said, "and distressed by the curse which hung over the family. I felt that Sir Henry should be warned of the terrible danger."

"I do not believe in such nonsense," said Watson. "If you meant no more, why did you not wish your brother to know what you said?"

"My brother is very anxious to have the Hall inhabited, for he thinks that it is for the good of the poor folk in the countryside."

She bade Watson goodbye, leaving him full of vague fears.

This incident and others bearing on the suspects or the area were being diligently reported by Watson in his letters to Holmes. He had told Holmes of the vast, desolate moor, and of the prehistoric stone huts and monoliths that dotted the low hillsides. In this connection he wrote in his letter of October 13th the latest news about the escaped convict. It appeared that the man had gotten away, for nothing had been seen or heard of him for a fortnight. While one of the stone huts would have given him shelter, there was nothing to eat on the moor but a moor sheep, which would have to be caught and slaughtered. The letter continued:

> *A dreadful place in the moor is where the legend of the wicked Hugo had its origin, some miles away from the Hall. We were taken there by Stapleton, who, when pressed by Sir Henry, told of other families that had suffered from an evil influence.*
>
> *We all went on to lunch at Merripit House, and from the first moment Sir Henry saw Miss Stapleton he appeared to be strongly attracted to her; I believe the feeling is mutual. Since then hardly a day has passed that we have not seen the brother and sister, but Stapleton is quite evidently opposed to such a match. He is much attached to his sister, but to prevent so brilliant a marriage would be most selfish of him.*

Watson wrote that at Sir Henry's request, Dr. Mortimer had taken the baronet, the Stapletons, and himself, to the yew alley to show them exactly how everything had occurred on that fatal night. And he had finally met Mr. Frankland of Lafter Hall, an elderly, red-faced, white-haired, choleric man, whose passion was the British law. Frankland had spent a fortune in litigation, and was presently involved in seven law suits. He had an excellent telescope on the roof of his house, and was spending many hours a day sweeping the moor in hopes of catching a glimpse of the escaped convict. He had provided comic relief where it was badly needed.

There was more to tell regarding the Barrymores:

> *I told Sir Henry about my visit to the Grimpen postmaster. He at once had Barrymore in to ask if he had received the telegram himself. Barrymore said that his wife had given it to him in the loft; he seemed taken aback by the question, and asked, 'Have I done something to forfeit your confidence?' Sir Henry assured him that he had not, and to pacify him, gave him some of his American clothes. I have seen Mrs. Barrymore tearful again; a deep sorrow gnaws at her heart.*
>
> *Last night at two in the morning I heard steps passing my room. Barrymore was walking stealthily down the corridor, carrying a candle. I followed him to the other wing. He entered an unfurnished room, and crouched at the window with the candle held against the glass. Then with an impatient gesture he put out the light. Long afterwards I heard a key turn somewhere in a lock. This morning I had a talk about the matter with Sir Henry, and we have planned a campaign.*

Watson's next letter to Holmes, written two days later, spelled out the unexpected results of the campaign.

> *The morning after I had followed Barrymore, I examined the room in which he had been. The western window through which he had stared commands the nearest outlook on to the moor through an opening between two trees. Sir Henry had also been aware that sometimes Barrymore walked about*

"Sir Henry had drawn Miss Stapleton to his side."

at night, and we agreed to do what we though you would have done—follow Barrymore and see what he was up to. Sir Henry felt sure that Barrymore would not hear us as he was somewhat deaf. But before I come to Barrymore, I must tell you what happened during the day concerning Sir Henry.

The baronet, Watson reported, was deeply infatuated with Miss Stapleton, and had arranged to meet her on the moor path. He had objected to Watson's accompanying him, despite Holmes's warning that he not go out alone. Placed in an awkard position, Watson had decided to follow Sir Henry secretly. From a hill, he had seen the couple in earnest conversation, and then, some distance away, Stapleton with his butterfly net moving in their direction. Sir Henry had drawn Miss Stapleton to his side, though she appeared to be straining away from him. At that instant Stapleton had come running towards them, gesticulating wildly. What looked like a vehement argument to Watson had taken place between Stapleton and Sir Henry. Finally, beckoning to his sister in a peremptory way, Stapleton had walked off with her by his side, leaving Sir Henry looking the picture of dejection. The letter went on:

I met Sir Henry on the path, and explained how I had witnessed all that had occurred.

'What's the matter with me, anyhow?' the bewildered baronet asked. 'Would I not make a good husband to a woman that I loved? What has Stapleton against me? Yet he would not let me touch the tips of his sister's fingers.'

'Did he say as much?' I asked.

'That, and a deal more. But she would not talk about love, either. She kept saying this was a place of danger, and she would never be happy until I left it. I told her if she wanted me to go, she would have to marry me and go with me. Before she could answer, along came Stapleton shouting like a madman that I leave his sister alone. I am badly puzzled.'

I was puzzled too, until Stapleton came that afternoon to offer apologies. Sir Sir Henry told me Stapleton had explained that his sister was everything to him; the thought of losing her was really terrible. He said he would withdraw all opposition if Sir Henry would be content with his sister's friendship for the next three months. Sir Henry gave him his promise, and we are to dine at Merripit House next Friday.

Returning to the story of the Barrymores, Watson reported that the first night after he had followed Barrymore and his candle, he and Sir Henry had sat for hours in Sir Henry's rooms, vainly waiting for Barrymore to pass. The next night, at two o'clock, they had heard steps in the corridor and had gone in pursuit. Barrymore had passed into the same room as before, candle in hand, and had gone to the window, and Sir Henry, followed by Watson, had walked in and confronted the frightened man. Watson recounted the scene:

'What are you doing here, Barrymore?' demanded Sir Henry.

'I was seeing if the window was fastened.'

'Look here, Barrymore,' said Sir Henry sternly. 'No lies! Come now, what were you doing at that window?'

'I was doing no harm, sir,' cried Barrymore, wringing his hands. 'Please, Sir Henry, don't ask me!'

'It must be a signal, Sir Henry,' I said. I held the candle as Barrymore had done, and stared into the darkness. 'There it is!' A pinpoint of yellow light was glowing in answer.

'Who is your confederate out yonder, and what is this conspiracy?' cried the baronet. 'Your family has lived with mine for a hundred years, and I find you plotting against me!'

'No, no, sir, not against you!' It was Mrs. Barrymore's voice. She stood horror-struck at the door. 'It is my doing, Sir Henry, all mine. He has done nothing but for my sake, and because I asked him.'

'Speak out, then! What does it mean?' cried Sir Henry.

What was the distraught Mrs. Barrymore's explanation of her husband's actions and the light on the moor? Did you deduce it?

Across

1 Yegg's target
5 Towel inscription
8 White poplar
13 Selves
14 French friends
16 Holy cup
17 Gator's cousin
18 Its capital is Bamako
19 Multitudes
20 Vichy
21 Atmospheric problem
22 ____ point of (about to)
23 Arithmetical sign
25 Versifier Ogden
27 Whalebone
30 Skilled in
34 Organic compound
35 Negri of the silents
36 Roué
37 Oil-well drilling equipment
38 Taken as a premise

39 Heater
40 Genuine: Ger.
42 Mimicked
43 Scenic view
45 Changed implements and dies
47 What's-his-name
48 Pestiferous child
49 City in France
50 "Tell me ____ is fancy bred"
53 Duos
55 Immense
59 Blood condition: Suffix
60 Apiece
61 Repellent: Slang
62 ". . . and, by a sleep to say ____"
63 Wild plum
64 ____ off the old block
65 Hits hard
66 Salt
67 Mal de ____

Down

1 Mems. of the Cabinet
2 Field: Comb. form
3 Provender
4 Skipped
5 Knut ____, Norwegian novelist
6 Moslem leaders
7 Grain tower
8 Horrified
9 "Big ____ is watching you"
10 ". . . somewheres ____ of Suez"
11 Nat. of Vilna
12 Otherwise
15 Gave the high sign
24 Light-Horse Harry
26 Sturdy ____ ox
27 Emptier
28 Priest's shawl
29 Kind of heavyweight
30 Stirred

31 Hindu melodies
32 Giraffes' kin
33 Entertains
35 Slender tubes
38 Celebration
41 ". . . never good ____ bad news"
43 "____ shall have music . . ."
44 Find guilty
46 Mountain nymphs
47 Partner of dryer
49 Pulverized chocolate
50 Arabic letters
51 Cad
52 Flightless Australian bird
54 Disney
56 Gnawing
57 Revue staple
58 Classify

Puzzle XVII: *Report of Dr. Watson*

Solution on page 158

——— ——— ——— ——— ———   ——— ——— ——— ——— ———   ——— ——— ——— ———

4 Down   44 Down   47 Down

——— ——— ——— ——— ——— ———;   ——— ——— ——   ——— ——— ——— ———

9 Down   5 Across   29 Down

——— ——— ——— ——— ——— ——— ———   ——— ——— ——— ——— ———   ——— ——— ——— ———

15 Down   50 Across   1 Across

——— ——   ——— ——— ——— ———   ——— ——— ——— ———.

41 Down   3 Down

Extract from the Diary of Dr. Watson

Sir Henry and Watson had stared in amazement at Mrs. Barrymore, continued Watson's letter, as she made her sad confession. Selden, the Notting Hill murderer, was her younger brother, much pampered in his childhood, who had grown up thinking the world was made for his pleasure. As he grew older, he had met wicked companions, and had gone from crime to crime, but to his loving sister he was always the curly-headed boy. Knowing that his sister lived near the prison, he had escaped and run to Baskerville Hall for shelter. Mrs. Barrymore and her husband had taken him in, but upon Sir Henry's arrival they thought he would be safer on the moor. Every second night, on seeing his signal, Barrymore had brought him bread and meat. Barrymore had corroborated his brokenhearted wife's story. The letter went on:

"Barrymore had corroborated his brokenhearted wife's story."

'Well, I cannot blame you for standing by your own wife,' said Sir Henry. 'Go to your room, now, you two.'

When they had gone, we looked out of the window again—a tiny point of light still glowed in the distance.

'I wonder he dares,' said Sir Henry.

'It may be so placed as to be only visible from here. I think it comes from the Cleft Tor, about a mile or so away.'

'By thunder,' said Sir Henry, 'I am going to take that man!'

I agreed with Sir Henry that it was our duty to put him back where he belonged, as he was a danger to the community. In five minutes we were on our way; I had taken my revolver, Sir Henry his hunting crop. Suddenly, out of the night came a rising howl, then a low, sad moan, sounding again and again.

'My God, Watson, what's that?' cried Sir Henry.

'It's a sound they have on the moor. I've heard it before.'

'It was the cry of a hound, Watson!' said the baronet. 'What do the folk on the countryside call this sound?'

'They say it is the cry of the Hound of the Baskervilles.'

'It came from the Grimpen Mire, did it not?'

'Stapleton said it might be the call of a strange bird.'

'No!' said Sir Henry. 'Can there be some truth in all these stories? Am I really in danger? You don't believe in the Hound, Watson, but that cry seemed to freeze my blood!'

Despite the terrifying sound, Watson wrote, young Baskerville would not give up the chase, and they found at last whence the convict's light came. A guttering candle had been stuck in a crevice of the rocks which flanked it on each side so as to keep the wind from it and also to prevent it from being visible, save in the direction of the Hall. Watson and Sir Henry had crouched behind a boulder, waiting, until over the rocks appeared an evil yellow face, all seamed and scored with vile passions. The convict had peered suspiciously around him, as if poised for flight. Sir Henry and Watson, fearing he would vanish, had sprung forward, but the stocky Selden, unexpectedly agile as a mountain goat, had eluded them. Watson would not shoot an unarmed fleeing man.

Then, as the disappointed men were making their way home, a most strange thing had occurred. Watson described it:

The moon was low, and the jagged pinnacle of a granite tor could be seen against this silver disc. There, outlined as black as ebony, was the figure of a tall, thin man upon the tor. It was not the convict—he was short and squat. With a cry of surprise I turned to grasp Sir Henry's arm to point the man out to him, but in that instant the man disappeared—Sir Henry had not seen him. I wanted to search the tor, but Sir Henry, whose nerves were still quivering from the eerie sound, was in no mood for fresh adventures.

'A warder, no doubt,' said he. 'The moor has been thick with them since the fellow escaped.'

111

We mean to communicate to the Princetown people where they should look for the escaped convict.

Watson had been sending detailed missives to Holmes regularly, but he had also been keeping a diary in which, in addition to recording facts and events, he had put down his thoughts and speculations about the case. In his entry of October 16th he wrote of the baronet's black mood and of his own feeling of impending danger. He speculated on the possibility of a live, huge hound inhabiting the moor. Where could such a hound lie concealed? Where did it get its food, where did it come from, how was it that no one saw it by day? But the man in the cab in London, and the warning letter to Sir Henry, had been real enough. Could the man in the cab be the stranger upon the tor? Watson had now met all the neighbors, and the man on the tor was not one of them.

In the same entry, Watson had also written about surprising information that had been volunteered by Barrymore. After breakfast that day, Barrymore had asked to speak to Sir Henry privately. Watson could hear raised voices in the study; after a time Sir Henry had called Watson in.

> *'Barrymore thinks it was unfair of us to hunt his brother-in-law down, when he, of his own free will, had told us the secret,' said Sir Henry. 'But, Barrymore, you, or rather your wife, told us only when you could not help yourself. The man is a public danger; he should be under lock and key.'*
>
> *'I assure you he will never trouble anyone in this country again, Sir Henry. In a few days arrangements will have been made to send him to South America. I beg of you, sir, not to let the police know he is still on the moor. He will not commit any more crimes—it would show where he was hiding.'*
>
> *'That is true,' said Sir Henry. 'Well, Barrymore—'*
>
> *'God bless you, sir, and thank you from my heart!'*
>
> *'That's an end of it, then—you can go.'*
>
> *Barrymore started to leave, then hesitated.*
>
> *'You have been so kind, sir, that I should like to do what I can for you. I know something about Sir Charles's death.'*
>
> *'What is it, then?' cried Sir Henry, jumping to his feet.*
>
> *'I know why he was at the gate at that hour. It was to meet a woman. I do not know her name. Her initials were L. L.'*
>
> *'How do you know this, Barrymore?'*
>
> *'Your uncle had only one letter that morning. It was from Coombe Tracey, and it was addressed in a woman's hand.'*

According to Barrymore, noted Watson in his diary, it had been his wife who found part of a charred letter while cleaning out the grate in Sir Charles's study; the discovery had occurred only a few weeks ago. The words that could be made out before the fragment crumbled were: "Please, please, as you are a gentleman, burn this letter, and be at the gate by ten o'clock." Beneath the words were the initials L. L. Sir Henry had then asked Barrymore why he had concealed the information. Barrymore had given two reasons: one, that the escape of Selden, taking place at just that time, had preoccupied his wife and himself; and two, they had been reluctant to disclose Sir Charles's involvement with a lady. Watson had immediately sent Holmes a report of this new development.

In his diary entry of October 17th, Watson wrote that his thoughts about the mysterious man on the tor had led him in the rainy evening to put on his waterproof and make his way to the craggy tor. From its summit, the only signs of life to be seen were the towers of Baskerville Hall and the stone huts on the hillsides. There was no trace of that lonely man he had seen two nights ago. Walking back, he had been overtaken by Dr. Mortimer driving in his dogcart, who had given him a lift homeward. Watson had asked him if he knew any woman whose initials were L. L., and the doctor, wrote Watson, had given a startling answer.

'No,' he said, 'there's no one with those initials. Wait a bit though,' he added after a pause, 'there's Laura Lyons—but she lives in Coombe Tracey. She's Frankland's daughter.'

'What! Old Frankland the crank?'

'Exactly. She married an artist named Lyons, who deserted her. Frankland would have nothing to do with her because she had married without his consent. She had had a pretty bad time. Her story got about, and Stapleton, Sir Charles, myself, and some others, set her up in a typewriting business.'

Tomorrow I shall go to Coombe Tracey, and if I can see this Mrs. Laura Lyons, a long step will have been made towards clearing one incident in this chain of mysteries.

Mortimer stayed to dinner, and he and Sir Henry played at cards afterwards. Barrymore brought my coffee to the library.

'Has this precious relation of yours departed?' I asked.

'I've not heard from him since I left food out three days ago. When next I went that way, the food was gone. I don't know if it was he or the other man who took it.'

'There's another man on the moor?' I gasped. 'Have you seen him?'

'No, sir.'

'How do you know of him then?'

How had Barrymore learned of the presence of another man on the moor?

Across

1 Obtuse
4 Solomon's successor
9 Kind of tea
13 Smell ____ (suspect a trick)
15 Roman official
16 "A load would sink a ____. . ."
17 Ethel, John and Lionel
19 Toilsome travel
20 Frightful sight
21 Exist in
23 Horse's hair
24 Asia, in Amiens
25 Pet pastime
28 Numskulls
30 "No ____ is an island . . ."
33 Of use, old style
34 Charge
35 Split
36 ". . . a lucky sixpence in her ____"
37 ____ up (misbehaved)

39 Old musical notes
40 Small barrels
41 ____-jongg
42 Gust of wind
43 Some upperclassmen: Abbr.
44 Challenges
46 Declaims wildly
47 Made known
48 Chesterfield, for example
50 Flogging
53 Prisoner
56 "Madam, I'm ____"
57 Deifications
60 Razz
61 Mme. Curie
62 Sioux State, for short
63 Othello was one
64 Malign
65 Crafty

Down

1 Small bit
2 "Dies ____"
3 "O ____, at thy window be!"
4 Evil spirit
5 Highly honored
6 Crossbow arrow
7 O'Neill one-acter
8 Left off
9 All ____ mind
10 Close attention
11 Invariably
12 Embankment
14 Shakes
18 Belgian violinist
22 City in Yugoslavia
24 Away from the wind
25 Shucks corn
26 The ____ day (recently)
27 Life stories, for short
29 At the top ____ ladder

30 Fine straw
31 Nautical interjection
32 Aeries
35 Kinship
37 Mercury alloys
38 Comical character
42 Lionhearted
44 Tutor at Oxford's Trinity
45 Caledonia
47 Stopwatch
49 "Rings ____ fingers . . ."
50 Injure
51 Personal: Comb. form
52 Wall border
53 Nuclear-reactor component
54 Degrees in Mary Baker Eddy's theology
55 Greenish blue
58 Jack of clubs
59 Firmament

Puzzle XVIII:
Extract from the Diary of Dr. Watson

1	2	3	■	4	5	6	7	8	■	9	10	11	12
13			14	15					■	16			
17			18						■	19			
■	20						■	21	22				
■		23				■	24				■	■	■
25	26	27			■	28	29				■	30	31	32
33					■		34			■	35			
36				■	37	38			■	39			
40			■	41			■	42					
43			■	44			45	46					
■		47				■	48	49			■	■	
50	51	52		■	53					54	55		■
56			■	57	58							59	
60			■	61				■	62			
63			■	64				■	65			

Solution on page 158

__ __ __ __ __ __ __ , __   __ __ __ __ __ __ __

17 Across   53 Across

__ __ __ __ __ __ __ __   __ __ __   __ __ __

35 Down   47 Across   29 Down

__ __ __ __   __ __ __   __ __ __ __ __   __ __   __ __ __

26 Down   30 Across   50 Across   9 Down

__ __ __ __ .

63 Across

The Man on the Tor

Watson's diary entry of October 17th continued with an account of his talk with Barrymore concerning the other man hiding in the moor.

'Selden told me of him a week ago or more,' said Barrymore. 'He's hiding, too, but he's not a convict. I don't like it, Dr. Watson—I tell you straight, sir, I don't like it!'

'Tell me frankly what it is that you don't like.'

'It's all these goings-on, sir! Look at Sir Charles's death. Look at the noises on the moor at night, and the stranger hiding out yonder, watching and waiting!'

'About this stranger—did Selden find out where he hid, or what he was doing?'

'Selden said he was a kind of gentleman, but he could not make out what he was doing there. He lives among the old stone huts on one of the hillsides.'

'But how about his food?'

'Selden found that he has got a lad who works for him, and brings all he needs—from Combe Tracey, most likely.'

'Very good, Barrymore. We may talk further another time.'

When Barrymore had gone, Watson walked over to the window, and looked out at the black, wild, windswept night. What hatred leads a man to lurk in such a place at such a time? Watson made up his mind that on the very next day he would look into the mysteries of the man on the tor and of Mrs. Lyons.

The next morning Watson asked Sir Henry if he wanted to go with him to Coombe Tracey to see Mrs. Lyons. Talking it over, they both decided that an informal visit by one person would elicit more information from the lady than a confrontation by two.

Perkins drove Watson to Coombe Tracey; they had no difficulty in finding Mrs. Lyons's rooms. A maid showed Watson into the well-appointed sitting-room office. Mrs. Lyons was a very handsome, brown-haired woman, with a touch of hardness in her face. Not pleased to see a stranger, she asked Watson why he had come.

"I have the pleasure," said Watson, "of knowing your father."

"I have nothing in common with him," she said. "If it were not for the late Sir Charles Baskerville and other kind hearts, I might have starved for all that my father cared."

"It is about Sir Charles that I have come to see you."

The lady started, then asked, "What can I tell you about him?"

"You knew him, did you not?"

"It is due to his interest that I am able to support myself."

"Did you correspond with him?"

"What is the object of these questions?" Mrs. Lyons asked angrily.

"To avoid public scandal."

Turning pale, she asked, "What do you want to know?"

"On what dates did you write to Sir Charles?"

"I wrote once or twice to thank him—I do not know the dates."

"Have you ever met him?"

"Yes, once or twice, when he came to Coombe Tracey."

"If you so seldom saw him or wrote to him, how did he know enough about your affairs to be able to help you?"

"Mr. Stapleton was kind enough to tell him."

"Did you ever write to Sir Charles asking him to meet you?"

"Certainly not," said Mrs. Lyons, flushing with anger.

"Your memory deceives you," said Watson. "I can quote a passage from your letter." He repeated the words Barrymore had revealed. "Sir Charles burned the letter, but that much was legible."

"Yes, I did write it!" she cried, now deathly pale. "I wished him to help me—I believed an interview would aid my cause."

"But why at such an hour?"

"Because I had just learned he was going away to London the next day. There were reasons why I could not get there earlier."

"Why a rendezvous outside instead of a visit to the house?"

"A woman cannot go alone at that hour to a bachelor's house."

"Well, what happened when you did get there?"

"I never went! A private matter prevented me. I swear by all I hold sacred, that is the truth!"

Watson questioned her again and again, but Mrs. Lyons insisted that she had not kept the appointment with Sir Charles.

"What was in the letter that you asked Sir Charles to burn?"

"It was a personal matter."

"If I have to call in the police," Watson warned, "you will find out how seriously you are compromised."

"I will tell you," she said at last. "My life has been an incessant persecution from a husband I abhor. The law is on his side; he may be able to force me to live with him again. I learned that I could regain my freedom if certain expenses could be met. I thought if Sir Charles heard the story from my own lips he would help me."

"Then how is it that you did not go to meet him?"

"Because I received help in the interval from another source."

"Why did you not write to Sir Charles and explain this?"

"I would have, had I not seen his death in the paper next morning."

Watson came away from the interview disheartened. Mrs. Lyons appeared to be telling the truth, but why had she acted so evasively? He would check her story by finding if she had instituted divorce proceedings about the time of Sir Charles's death.

Turning to his second quest, the man on the tor, Watson noted, as he drove back along the highroad with Perkins, that hundreds of stone huts were scattered over the hills. But as he had seen the man on the Black Tor, he decided he would start his search there.

Luck came to his aid in the person of Mr. Frankland, who was standing at his highroad gate when Watson drove into view.

"Good day, Dr. Watson," he cried. "You must give your horses a rest, and come in to have a glass of wine and congratulate me."

Watson sent Perkins and the wagonette home, and followed Frankland into his dining room.

"I have closed the wood where the Fernworthy folk used to picnic," said Frankland gleefully. "These infernal people think there are no rights to property, and that they can swarm where they like. I act entirely from a sense of public duty, but I have no doubt that the Fernworthy people will burn me in effigy tonight. The County Constabulary is in a scandalous state—they did not stop the burning last time they did it. I told the police they would have occasion to regret their treatment of me, and my words have come true!"

"How so?" asked Watson.

"I could tell them what they are dying to know, but nothing would induce me to help them. It's about the convict on the moor."

"You don't mean you know where he is?"

"I know how to find him. The way to catch a man is to find out where he gets his food and trace it to him. I have seen with my own eyes the messenger who takes him his food." As Watson's heart sank for Barrymore, Frankland continued, "His food is taken to him by a boy. I see him every day through my telescope."

"He may be the son of a moorland shepherd taking out his father's dinner," said Watson, hoping to draw Frankland out.

"Do you see the Black Tor over yonder?" asked Frankland. "And do you see the low hill beyond with the thornbush on it—the stoniest part of the moor? Is that a place for a shepherd's station? But wait a moment—isn't there something moving on the hillside? Come, sir, come! You will see with your own eyes."

Frankland rushed up to his roof, followed by Watson. He clapped his eye to the telescope and gave a cry of satisfaction.

"Quick, Dr. Watson, quick, before he passes over the hill!"

Watson could see a small urchin carrying a little bundle.

"Well, am I right?" cried Frankland. "But not a word shall the police have from me. I bind you to secrecy too, Dr. Watson!"

"Just as you wish," said Watson.

He resisted Frankland's invitation to stay longer, and was soon on his way to the stony hill. The sun was sinking when he reached its summit. The boy was nowhere to be seen, but beneath him, in a cleft of the hills, was a circle of stone huts, and in the middle was one which had retained sufficient roof to act as a screen against the weather. At last, the stranger's secret was within his grasp!

"He clapped his eye to the telescope."

Watson approached the hut warily—all was silent within. Closing his hand on the butt of his revolver, he looked in at the door. The place was empty, but there were ample signs that it had been inhabited—blankets, cooking utensils, food tins. Then, on a flat stone, he saw a sheet of paper with writing on it. The scrawl, roughly pencilled, said: "Dr. Watson has gone to Coombe Tracey."

It was he, then, and not Sir Henry, who was being dogged by this secret man! He looked around for other reports, but there were none. Nor were there any signs to indicate the character or intentions of the man, save that he must be of Spartan habits. Thinking of the heavy rains and looking at the gaping roof, Watson understood how strong and immutable must be the purpose that kept the man in this inhospitable abode.

The sun had sunk low, and with tingling nerves, Watson sat in the darkened hut waiting for its tenant. At last he heard him! As the footsteps came nearer and nearer, he shrank back and cocked the pistol in his pocket. Then a shadow fell across the opening of the hut, and a voice spoke.

Can you guess what the voice said, and to whom it belonged?

Across

1 Aircraft section
5 Hilo hello
10 ___ *the Best?*
12 Wisconsin city
14 Slow gait
15 Slight, as a chance
17 Altitudes: Abbr.
18 Ending for rim or verb
19 Crete's Mount ___
20 "Oh, give ___ home . . ."
21 Slippery ___ eel
23 Put in words
25 Dens
27 Gift recipient
29 Fling here and there
31 Emerald, for one
32 Strive
34 Oliver Wendell
36 Branch of Brit. armed forces

37 First half of an inning
38 Pleasing to the eye
42 Kind of buoy
47 ___ even keel
48 It measures 16,900,000 sq. mi.
50 Brittle
51 Musical note
53 Show up
55 "___ mad world"
56 Zero
57 Early Babylonian god
59 Librarian's degree
61 Cyst
62 Visionary
64 Leveling off
66 Words in a letter salutation
67 Papal ambassador
68 Expression of apology
69 Second-year student

Down

1 ___ so (this way)
2 Author Rand
3 Division word
4 Fertile soil
5 Cuckoopints, for example
6 Sound the praises of
7 Based on the number eight
8 ". . . ___ terrible, swift sword"
9 Belief in spirits, demons, etc.
10 DNA scientist
11 Deal with
13 She swam English Channel
14 Phantom
16 Comforts
22 Born
24 Suffix for infer or inter
26 "O, what can ___ thee. . ."
28 British nobleman
30 Abode for a certain old woman
33 ___ con Dios

35 Assoc. including Saudi Arabia, Kuwait, etc.
37 Shackle
38 ___ behold!
39 ___ ground (supported by facts)
40 Dales
41 Alfonso XIII's queen
42 Life: Comb. form
43 Dernier ___
44 Make a ___ (take the fancy of)
45 Ancient Hebrew ascetic
46 Smack-dab
49 Skedaddle
52 More docile
54 Pixies
58 Intimate
60 Utah State flower
63 Commotion
65 Pile

Puzzle XIX: *The Man on the Tor*

Solution on page 159

"___ ___, __ __ __ ___ _____ _____,

55 Across   38 Across   64 Across

___ _____ _____. _____ ___

66 Across   10 Down   10 Across

_____ _____ _____?" _____ _____.

53 Across 15 Across   23 Across   34 Across

Death on the Moor

H olmes!" cried Watson, hardly able to believe his ears.
Stepping outside, he found Holmes sitting on a stone, looking thin and worn, but alert, and as trim and clean-shaven as ever.

"I was never more glad or surprised to see anyone in my life!" said Watson.

"The surprise was not all yours," said Holmes. "I had no idea you had found my retreat until I saw a Bradley cigarette butt over there. You saw me the night you and Sir Henry were hunting Selden?"

"Yes," said Watson, "and your boy was observed by Frankland."

"My boy Cartwright," said Holmes. He peeped into the hut and fetched out the sheet of paper. "So you have been to Coombe Tracey? To see Mrs. Lyons, no doubt. Our researches have been parallel."

"You led me to think you were in London," said Watson, disappointed. "You see me, and yet you do not trust me."

"Had I been with you and Sir Henry, my point of view would have been the same as yours, and my presence would have warned our opponents. I have been able to get around more than I could have, had I stayed at the Hall."

"Then my reports have all been wasted!" cried Watson.

"No, they are well thumbed," said Holmes, taking them out of his pocket. "I made arrangements for their delivery. I must compliment you on your zeal and intelligence. Now, tell me about Mrs. Lyons."

The air had turned chill; Holmes and Watson went into the hut, where Watson related his conversation with the lady.

"You have filled a gap I had been unable to bridge," said Holmes. "You are aware, perhaps, that a close intimacy exists between Mrs. Lyons and Stapleton. If I could only use it to detach his wife—"

"His wife!" exclaimed Watson.

"Miss Stapleton is in reality his wife."

"How could he have permitted Sir Henry to fall in love with her!"

"He took particular care that Sir Henry did not *make* love to her."

"But why this elaborate deception?"

"He foresaw that she would be more useful in her pose as a free woman."

"It is he, then, who is our enemy—who dogged us in London?"

"So I read the riddle. And the warning came from her."

"But how do you know, Holmes, that the woman is his wife?"

"I traced him through a bit of autobiography he gave you—he had owned a school in the north which closed under peculiar circumstances. The owner— he had a different name—and his wife disappeared. Their descriptions matched the Stapletons', including the man's interest in entomology."

"If this woman is his wife, where does Mrs. Lyons come in?"

"I did not know until you told me that she was contemplating divorce. Regarding Stapleton as an unmarried man, she no doubt is counting on marrying him. We must see her—both of us—tomorrow."

"What is the meaning of it all? What is Stapleton after?"

"It is murder, Watson. But my nets are closing upon him, even as his are upon Sir Henry. There is but one danger—if he should strike before we do."

Suddenly, a terrible, anguished scream burst out of the moor.

"My God!" gasped Watson. "What is it?"

Holmes had sprung to his feet, and was peering into the darkness. The cry burst on their ears, nearer, louder than before.

"Where is it?" Holmes whispered. "Where is it, Watson?"

"There, I think," said Watson, pointing into the darkness.

Again the agonized cry swept through the silent night, louder and still nearer. And a new, low, menacing sound mingled with it.

"The hound!" cried Holmes. "Come, Watson, come!"

Holmes started running wildly over the moor, with Watson at his heels. But now there came one despairing yell, and then a dull, heavy thud. They halted and listened. All was silent.

"He has beaten us! We are too late! Fool that I was to hold my hand. And you, Watson, see what comes of abandoning your charge!"

Blindly they ran through the gloom, blundering against boulders. Then a low moan reached their ears, coming from their left. On that side a ridge of rocks ended in a cliff which overlooked a stone-strewn slope. On the slope a prostrate man lay face downward, spread-eagled. They ran down and stooped over the figure. Holmes lit a match; it shone on the crushed skull and the body of Sir Henry Baskerville, and on his ruddy tweed suit. The match flickered and died, even as hope died for Holmes and Watson.

"Oh, Holmes," cried Watson, "I shall never forgive myself."

Holmes groaned. "I am more to blame than you. In order to have my case complete, I have thrown away the life of my client."

"Where is this brute hound? Where is Stapleton?" cried Watson.

"He shall answer for his deed," said Holmes. "Uncle and nephew have been murdered—the one frightened to death by the sight of the beast, the other driven to his end in his wild flight to escape from it. But now we have to prove the connection between the man and the beast. We cannot even swear to the existence of the hound, since Sir Henry has died from the fall off the cliff."

They stood with bitter hearts beside the mangled body. Then as the moon rose they climbed to the top of the rocks. No life stirred on the moor, but they saw, far off, the lights of Merripit House.

"Why should we not seize Stapleton at once?" asked Watson.

"Our case is not complete. If we make one false move the villain may escape us—he is wary and cunning to the last degree. Now we must perform the last offices for our poor friend."

They made their way down the slope, and approached the body.

"We must send for help, Holmes; we cannot carry him all the way to the Hall. Good Heavens, are you mad?"

Holmes had uttered a great cry as he bent over the moonlit body.

From the clues, can you deduce what caused Holmes to cry out?

Across

1 ____ fool of
6 Kind of center
10 Beat all hollow
14 James or George
15 French priest
16 Lagomorph
17 Clerical vestment
18 Metric measure (32.808 ft.)
20 ____ Galahad
21 Not hold ____ to
23 John Bull, for short
24 ____-Magnon
25 Access
27 Nothing to brag about
30 Judaic candelabra
34 Square
35 Companion of wife
36 Civet's cousin
40 Crust
42 Me, in Marseille
43 Swelling
44 Lag behind
45 I love, in Latin
46 Play-script direction
47 Card game
50 Ending for kitchen or luncheon
51 Expedient
54 ____es Salaam
56 Hoopla
57 Sprucer
61 Particle of negation
64 Brutal
66 "If ____ a King"
68 Gamble or gambol
69 Miscalculates
70 Costly fur
71 "____ right with the world"
72 Repudiate
73 Ruhr-valley city

Down

1 Electrical units
2 Gas: Comb. form
3 Wood knot
4 ____king (evil spirit)
5 ". . . for ____ and a day"
6 Art movement
7 Scrooge's nickname
8 Before e, f, g . . .
9 Vegas VIP
10 Definite article
11 Estimator
12 Castle or Rich
13 Combine
19 Household
22 U.S. Navy off.
24 Prove culpable
26 "Where ____ and the antelope play"
27 Dispatched
28 More than
29 Antitoxins
31 Bovary and Eames
32 Ruth's mother-in-law
33 Shallot
37 Barbershop call
38 Discharge
39 London museum
41 The "lily maid of Astolat"
48 Filled with fear
49 Poem by Pindar
51 Florida seaport
52 ". . . no play makes Jack ____ boy"
53 Yellowish red
55 Come into being
58 Dashed
59 Pivot
60 Suburb of Paris
61 Bird bills
62 Heraldic border
63 Adolescent
65 Impaired: Prefix
67 "When I ____ a lad . . ."

Puzzle XX: *Death on the Moor*

Solution on page 159

_ _ _   _ _ _ _   _ _ _ _   _ _ _   _ _ _ _
10 Down   6 Across   35 Across   67 Down   10 Down

_ _ _ _ _ _ _ _ _   _ _ _ _ _ _ _ _ _ ,   _ _ _ _
64 Across   24 Down   61 Across

_ _ _ _   _ _ _ _ _ _ .
20 Across   14 Across

Fixing the Nets

A beard, a beard!" cried Holmes. "The man has a beard! It is not the baronet—it is, why, it is my neighbor, the convict!"

With feverish haste they had turned the body over. There could be no doubt to Watson that it was the same face which had glared upon him in the light of the candle from over the rocks—the evil face of Selden. He remembered that Sir Henry had given Barrymore some of his clothes, and Barrymore must have passed them on to help Selden in his escape.

"The clothes have been the poor devil's death," said Holmes. "The hound had been laid on by an article of Sir Henry's—the boot which was taken in the hotel, in all probability. The immediate problem is what to do with this poor wretch's body. Halloa, Watson, who is this coming? It's the man himself. Not a word to show our suspicions—or my plans crumble to the ground."

The dapper figure of Stapleton was approaching over the moor. He stopped when he saw Holmes and Watson, then came on again.

"Why, Dr. Watson, that's not you, is it? But what's this? Somebody hurt? Don't tell me that it is our friend Sir Henry!"

He stooped over the dead man—the cigar fell from his hand.

"Who—who's this?" he stammered.

"It's Selden, the man who escaped from Princetown."

Stapleton did his best to overcome his disappointment.

"Dear me! What a shocking affair! How did he die?"

"It appears that he fell over the rocks," said Watson. "My friend and I were strolling on the moor when we heard a cry."

"I heard a cry also. That was what brought me here. I was uneasy about Sir Henry, because I had suggested that he come over tonight. By the way—did you hear anything else besides a cry?"

"No," said Holmes. "Did you?"

"No, but you know the stories the peasants tell about a phantom hound. I was wondering if there were such a sound tonight."

"We heard nothing of the kind," said Watson.

"And what is your theory about this poor fellow's death?"

"Anxiety and exposure probably drove him off his head. He rushed about the moor in a crazy state, and fell over here."

"What do you think about it, Mr. Sherlock Holmes?"

"You are quick at identification," said Holmes, bowing.

"We have been expecting you since Dr. Watson came down. You are in time to see a tragedy."

"Yes, indeed. I agree with my friend's explanation of Selden's death. I take an unpleasant remembrance back to London tomorrow."

"Oh, you return tomorrow?" asked Stapleton. "I hope your visit has cast some light on our puzzling occurrences here."

"I need facts, not rumors. It has not been a satisfactory case."

The three men decided to cover Selden's face until he could be moved in the morning, and Stapleton took his leave.

Walking back to the Hall, Holmes remarked to Watson, "What nerves the fellow has! And we can prove nothing against him now. What signs are there of a hound? We heard it, but we could not prove it was after Selden. There is a complete absence of motive."

At the Hall gates, Watson asked, "Are you coming in, Holmes?"

"Yes, I see no need for further concealment. Say nothing of the hound to Sir Henry. Let him think Selden's death was an accident. He will have better nerve for the ordeal ahead of him tomorrow, when, if I remember your report, he dines with the Stapletons."

"I shall be dining with them, too."

"You must excuse yourself; he must go alone."

Sir Henry was pleased to see Holmes, but he did raise his eyebrows at Holmes's lack of luggage or any explanation for its absence. Watson had the sad duty of breaking the news of Selden's death to Barrymore and his wife.

At a belated supper Holmes told Sir Henry of Selden's accident. He was relieved to learn from the baronet that the clothes Selden had worn had no markings on them that would make them traceable. During the supper Sir Henry remarked that he had had a message from Stapleton asking him over, but that he had not gone because of Holmes's warning to him that he not go out alone. Sir Henry had asked Holmes about the progress of the case, and Holmes had just begun to reply, when he stopped suddenly and stared fixedly over Watson's head, into the air.

"What is it?" both Sir Henry and Watson cried.

"Excuse the admiration of a connoisseur," said Holmes, as he waved his hand toward the line of portraits which covered the opposite wall. "They are all family portraits, I presume? Do you know their names?"

"Barrymore has been teaching me—I think I know them."

"Who is the Cavalier opposite me, in black velvet and lace?"

"Ah, he is the cause of all the mischief, the wicked Hugo."

"Dear me," said Holmes. "I pictured him as more robust."

"There's no doubt about the authenticity of the painting, for the name and the date, 1647, are on the back of the canvas."

The picture of the old roysterer seemed to have a fascination for Holmes, for his eyes were continually fixed upon it during supper. Later, when Sir Henry had gone to his room, Holmes led Watson back to the dining room, and held his candle up to the time-stained portrait on the wall.

"Do you see anything there? Is it like anyone you know?"

"There is something of Sir Henry about the jaw," said Watson.

"Wait an instant." Holmes stood on a chair, and with his right arm covered the broad hat and the long ringlets of the Cavalier.

" 'Good heavens!' " cried Watson.

"Good heavens!" cried Watson, as the face of Stapleton sprang out of the canvas. "This is marvelous. It might be his portrait!"

"The fellow is a Baskerville—that is evident," said Holmes.

"With designs upon the succession," said Watson.

"Exactly. This picture has supplied us with one of our most obvious missing links. We have him, Watson, we have him!"

Though Watson had risen early the following morning, Holmes was afoot earlier still—Watson saw him coming up the drive.

"I sent a report from Grimpen to Princetown as to the death of Selden," said Holmes. "And I was also in touch with my faithful Cartwright."

"And what is the next move?"

"To see Sir Henry. Ah, here he is! You are invited, as I understand it, to dine with our friends the Stapletons tonight."

"I am sure they would want you to come also," said Sir Henry.

"I fear that Watson and I must go to London," said Holmes. The baronet's face showed his hurt at this desertion. "We shall leave after breakfast. Watson, please send your regrets to Stapleton."

"I have a good mind to go with you," said Sir Henry.

"You must stay here," said Holmes. "Drive to Merripit House, but send back your trap, and let them know you intend to walk home."

"To walk across the moor? But you cautioned me not to do that!"

"This time you will be safe—but as you value your life, go along the straight path from Merripit House to the Grimpen Road."

A few hours later Holmes and Watson drove to the station of Coombe Tracey, where they found Cartwright waiting for them.

"You will take this train to London, Cartwright, and as soon as you arrive you will send a wire to Sir Henry in my name, to say that if he finds my pocketbook he is to send it to Baker Street. And now ask at the station office if there is a message for me."

The boy returned with a telegram from Inspector Lestrade saying that he would arrive at five-forty with an unsigned warrant.

"This is in answer to mine of this morning. Now, Watson, we cannot employ our time better than by calling on Mrs. Laura Lyons."

Mrs. Lyons was in her office, and Holmes spoke frankly to her.

"I am investigating the circumstances of Sir Charles Baskerville's death. Dr. Watson, here, has informed me of what you told him, and also of what you have withheld concerning the matter."

"What have I withheld?" Mrs. Lyons asked defiantly.

"The connection between the time and place of the appointment you asked for, and Sir Charles's death at the same time and place. We regard this case as one of murder, and the evidence may implicate not only your friend Stapleton but his wife as well."

"His wife!" she cried. "His wife! He is not a married man. Prove it to me! And if you can do so—" Her eyes flashed.

"Here is a photograph of the couple," said Holmes, "taken four years ago in York, indorsed 'Mr. and Mrs. Vandeleur.' You will recognize the Stapletons. Here are written descriptions, by trustworthy witnesses, of the Vandeleurs who kept St. Oliver's private school in York. Read them, and see if you can doubt their identity."

Mrs. Lyons glanced at them, then looked up, a desperate woman.

"Mr. Holmes," she said, "this man offered me marriage on condition that I get a divorce. He has lied to me! I see that I was a tool in his hands. Why should I preserve faith with him? Ask me what you like. I swear I meant no harm to Sir Charles, who was my kind friend."

"I believe you," said Holmes. "This is very painful to you. I can make it easier by telling you what occurred, and you can tell me if I make mistakes. Stapleton suggested sending the letter?"

"He dictated it."

"He said you would receive money from Sir Charles for your divorce."

"Exactly."

"And then after you had sent the letter he dissuaded you from keeping the appointment. And when you learned of Sir Charles's death, he asked you not to say anything about your letter."

"Yes."

"How did he convince you to do what he wanted?" asked Holmes.

1) To dissuade Mrs. Lyons from keeping her appointment with Sir Charles, what did Stapleton promise to do? 2) To persuade her to say nothing about her letter, what did Stapleton warn her to do?

Across

1 Coal mines
5 "___ be not proud . . ."
10 Gives leave
14 Scotto specialty
15 Result
16 Baal, for one
17 Nexus
19 ___ qua non
20 Some
21 Greek god of war
22 Cleared as profit
24 River to the Elbe
25 Answer to a roll call
26 Prince of Wales
29 Sarcastic
32 Syrupy
33 Yoo-hoos!
34 Where unclaimed letters go: Abbr.
36 A.c. or d.c.
37 Join together

38 Opposite of aweather
39 Sunshine State, for short
40 Moslem ruler
42 Takes a flyer
44 Noah's landing place
46 Separate
47 Allies' commander in chief (1918)
48 ". . . the playing fields of ___"
49 "You get what you ___'"
52 Years, in the Apennines
53 Letter salutation
56 Oil: Comb. form
57 Brought round to
60 ___ Wars
61 Humors
62 Frog's cousin
63 ___ up (badly off)
64 Margins
65 Equal to

Down

1 South American rodent
2 Kind of Age
3 Diminutive
4 Angelo or Antonio
5 Ordained
6 Affiliates with
7 Sale condition
8 Your: It.
9 Poultry place
10 "___ to the Mockingbird"
11 Redact
12 Timbre
13 Coaster
18 Two under par
23 Aphrodite's son
24 ___ the Red
25 Hastened
26 Maestro of the kitchen
27 Shout of greeting
28 Have ___ to the ground
30 Time waster

31 French office worker
33 "Age cannot wither ___ . . ."
35 Bacteriologist's wire loop
37 Have done ___
38 Dramatic conflict
40 Slangy suffix
41 Lace of knotted cord
42 See personally
43 Steer clear of
45 Have the means for
46 Lay bare
49 Elegant
50 Canadian prov.
51 Word with solar or lunar
52 Eagerly expectant
53 Name-dropper
54 Type of type: Abbr.
55 ___ herd on (kept in line)
58 Staff
59 Give ___ whirl

Puzzle XXI: *Fixing the Nets*

Solution on page 160

1) __ __ __ __   __ __ __ __   __ __ __ __   __ __ __ __ __ __ __ __.
   49 Across   33 Down   46 Across

2) __ __ __ __ __   __ __ __ __   __ __ __ __ __ __ __ __ __ __
   43 Down   20 Across   17 Across

__ __ __ __ __ __ __   __ __ __ __ __ __ __ __ __ __ ' __ __ __ __ __ __.
37 Down   53 Across 26 Across   5 Across

131

The Hound of the Baskervilles

Mrs. Laura Lyons explained to Sherlock Holmes and Watson just how Stapleton had contrived to control her actions.

"He told me not to keep the appointment with Sir Charles, as it would hurt his self-respect if any other man should pay for my divorce—he would do it himself, poor though he was. When I read about Sir Charles's death, he said the death was a mysterious one, and that I should certainly be suspected if the facts came out."

"I think on the whole you have had a fortunate escape," said Holmes. "You have had him in your power and he knew it, and yet you are alive. We must wish you good morning now, Mrs. Lyons."

Holmes and Watson were at the station at Coombe Tracey when the 5:40 express roared in, and the small, wiry Lestrade alighted.

After they all shook hands, Lestrade asked, "Anything good?"

"The biggest thing in years," said Holmes. "But we have two hours before we start, time for dinner."

It was Holmes's habit to keep his plans to himself until the instant of their fulfillment. So Watson and Lestrade were not sure of their destination as they drove at eight o'clock towards the Hall. Holmes ordered the carriage to stop at the Hall gate and return to Coombe Tracey. The three men then started to walk to Merripit House.

"Are you armed, Lestrade?" asked Holmes. "Good! My friend and I are also ready for emergencies."

"You're mighty close about this affair, Mr. Holmes," said the inspector. "What's the game now?"

"A waiting game."

"My word, it doesn't seem a very cheerful place," said Lestrade, as they walked on. He shivered, glancing round at the gloomy slopes, and at the huge lake of fog which lay over the Grimpen Mire.

"The lighted house ahead is Merripit House, and the end of our journey," said Holmes. "I caution you not to talk above a whisper."

They stopped about two hundred yards from the house.

"We shall make our little ambush here, behind these rocks," said Holmes. "Can you tell the position of the rooms, Watson?"

"The latticed windows are the kitchen windows, and the brightly lit room is the dining room," said Watson.

"The blinds are up. Creep forward and see what they are doing."

Watson crept up to the low wall which surrounded the orchard. From there he could see that there were only two people in the dining room, Sir Henry and Stapleton. As he watched, Stapleton rose and left the room, while Sir Henry puffed on his cigar. Watson heard a door creak, and the sound of boots on gravel. Looking over, he saw Stapleton walk to an outhouse in the orchard, turn a key in the lock, and enter; a scuffling sound came from within. Stapleton was inside only a minute or so before he returned to the house.

Watson crept back and reported what he had seen.

"You say, Watson, that the lady is not there?" asked Holmes. "Where can she be, since there is no light in any other room except the kitchen?"

"I cannot think where she is," said Watson.

The dense white fog that hung over the Grimpen Mire was drifting slowly in the direction of Merripit House. The moon shone on it, making it look like a shimmering ice field.

"The fog is moving towards us," muttered Holmes. "The one thing which could disarrange my plans! It's already ten o'clock—Sir Henry should be coming out. His life may depend on it!"

Every minute the white fog drifted closer and closer to the house. Holmes struck his hand passionately on the rock in front of him.

"If he isn't out in a quarter of an hour the path will be covered. In half an hour we won't see our hands in front of us!"

As the fog bank flowed onward, Holmes and his companions fell back until they were half a mile from the house.

"We are going too far," said Holmes. "We must stop here." He put his ear to the ground. "Thank God, I hear him coming."

A sound of quick steps broke the silence of the moor. As they watched, Sir Henry emerged from the fog into the moonlight. Then he came swiftly along the path, and went on past them.

"Hist!" said Holmes, cocking his pistol. "Look out! It's coming!"

A continuous patter came from somewhere in the fog bank. Suddenly, Holmes froze in amazement, and at the same instant Lestrade yelled in terror and threw himself on the ground; Watson stood paralyzed. The dreadful shape that sprang out from the fog was a hound, enormous, coal black, but one such as mortal eyes have never seen. Fire burst from its open mouth, its eyes glowed, its muzzle and hackles and dewlap were outlined in flickering flames.

With long bounds the huge creature was following hard on Sir Henry's footsteps. So stunned were the three men by the apparition that they allowed it to pass before they recovered their nerve. Then Holmes and Watson both fired together, and the hound gave a hideous howl. One bullet at least had hit him, but he bounded onward. Holmes ran madly in pursuit, the others after. They heard Sir Henry's screams, and the deep roar of the hound. They were in time to see the beast spring on its victim, hurl him to the ground, and worry at his throat. But the next instant Holmes had killed the beast, emptying five barrels into its flank.

Sir Henry lay insensible where he had fallen. They tore away his collar, and Holmes breathed a prayer of gratitude—there was no wound. Then the baronet stirred and opened his eyes.

"My God!" he whispered. "What was it?"

"It's dead," said Holmes. "We've laid the family ghost!"

The dead creature, which appeared to be a combination of bloodhound and mastiff, still seemed to drip with a bluish flame. Watson placed his hand on the glowing muzzle, and his own fingers smoldered and gleamed in the darkness.

"Phosphorus," he said.

"A cunning preparation of it," said Holmes, sniffing at the animal. "No smell to hinder the beast's power of scent. We owe you a deep apology, Sir Henry, for having exposed you to this danger."

"You have saved my life," said Sir Henry.

"We must leave you here," said Holmes. "If you will wait, one of us will go back with you to the Hall. But now the rest of our work must be done. We have our case, and now we want our man."

Before starting the search of the moor, Holmes led Watson and Lestrade back to Merripit House to make sure Stapleton was not there. The front door was open. Rushing in, they hurried from room to room, to the amazement of the old manservant. On the upper floor they came to a locked room, from which a faint moan sounded. Holmes struck the door with his foot, and it flew open. An object so unexpected faced them that they stood still, astonished.

The walls of the room were lined with glass cases full of butterflies and moths. In the center of the room was an upright beam, placed there to shore up the worm-eaten roof. To this post was tied a figure, swathed and muffled with sheets; only the eyes showed. Springing into action, the three men tore the bindings off, and Mrs. Stapleton sank to the floor before them. As her head fell, the red weal of a whiplash could be seen cross her neck.

"The brute!" cried Holmes. "Here, Lestrade, your brandy."

She opened her eyes, and they put her in a chair.

"Has Sir Henry escaped?" she asked. "Is he safe?"

"Yes," said Holmes, "and the hound is dead."

"Thank God!" she said, sighing with relief. "Oh, the villain! These marks are nothing! It is my mind and soul that he has tormented and defiled. I could endure it all if I knew I had his love, but now I know I have only been his dupe!"

She broke into passionate sobbing.

"Tell us then where we shall find him," said Holmes. "If you have ever aided him in his evil, help us now and so atone."

"There is an old tin mine on an island in the heart of the Grimpen Mire. It was there he kept his hound, and made preparations so that he might have a refuge. That is where he would fly."

"No one could find his way in there in this fog," said Holmes.

"He may find his way in, but never out," she cried. "How can he see the guiding wands we planted to mark the pathway?"

It was evident that pursuit would be vain until the fog lifted. Meanwhile Lestrade was left at the house, while Holmes and Watson went back with the baronet to the Hall. The story of the Stapletons could no longer be withheld from him. He took the blow bravely when he learned the truth about the woman he had loved. But the night's adventures had shattered his nerves, and before morning he lay delirious with fever. It would take many months before Sir Henry would become once again the hale, hearty man he had been.

The fog had lifted the next morning, and Mrs. Stapleton guided Holmes and his companions to where the pathway through the bog began. They left her standing on a peninsula of peaty soil that tapered out into the bog. Small wands planted here and there showed where the path zigzagged from tuft to tuft of rushes among the foul quagmires. The mire plucked at their heels as they walked. Holmes took a risk by reaching to retrieve a black object lying on a small tuft of grass. It was an old black boot, with the word "Toronto" printed inside—Sir Henry's missing boot!

"We know at least that he came this far safely," said Holmes.

There was no chance of finding footsteps in the mire, but coming to firmer ground beyond the morass, they looked eagerly for them.

What did Holmes and his companions find beyond the morass?

"It was an old black boot."

Across

1 ". . . I ___ out for stars"
4 Product of Mount Pelée
8 ". . . took ___ and went to sea"
13 Canvass
14 Mine entrance
15 Day or union
16 Part of Hamlet's question
17 ___ Mall
18 Companion of here
19 Resources
21 Build up in layers
23 Truth of the matter
25 Owned
26 Billiard stroke
29 Bishops' peaked caps
32 Make: Suffix
33 Soc.
35 Peers
39 Market place

41 Penetrated the mind
42 Kind of egg
43 ___ bene
45 "___ were a Queen"
46 Lured
48 Doctrine
50 Wide Sts.
53 Upper legislative branches
55 Stair
58 Fish hawk
62 Actor Hardy, to friends
63 Aviator's stunt
65 Underdone
66 Playing marble
67 A- or H-bomb: Slang
68 ". . . the wind ___ the palm trees"
69 Puccini heroine
70 Gravel ridges
71 ___ *Tempest*

Down

1 Presses one's suit
2 Priests' robes
3 Icy rains
4 Slip of the tongue
5 Nabakov novel
6 Hissers' target
7 Finally
8 High: Comb. form
9 German road
10 African sorcery
11 Main heart artery
12 Cornered
13 School org.
20 ___ of the absurd
22 Barest
24 Military trials, for short
26 Bog down
27 ___ Minor
28 Red and Black
30 Regards as identical

31 Center of a planetary system
34 Most painful
36 Similar
37 It isn't all beer and skittles
38 Fit of anger
40 British business abbr.
43 Stump
44 Go ___ spree
47 "___ more, my lady"
49 ___ de corps
50 Frothing
51 Europe's longest river
52 Gannet
54 Rise high
56 Josip Broz
57 "Mine eyes have ___ . . ."
59 Incautious
60 New York canal
61 Longing
64 Orel's river

Puzzle XXII:
The Hound of the Baskervilles

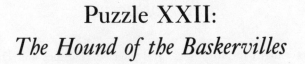

Solution on page 160

——— ——— ——— ——— —— — —— ——— —— — —
18 Across   1 Across   43 Across   55 Across

—— —— ——— ; ——— ——— ——— —— —
16 Across   57 Down   6 Down   25 Across

——— —— ——— ——— .
41 Across   71 Across 26 Down

A Retrospection

It was a raw night in November, and Sherlock Holmes and Dr. Watson sat on either side of a blazing fire in their sitting room in Baker Street. Holmes was in excellent spirits, having successfully concluded two important cases since the tragic affair in Devonshire, so Watson was able to induce him to discuss the Baskerville mystery.

"The course of events," said Holmes, "from Stapleton's point of view was simple and direct, but to us, not knowing his motives at the start, it appeared complex. I have spoken with Mrs. Stapleton, and my notes on the entire matter are in my indexed list of cases."

"Perhaps you would give me a sketch of it from memory."

"My inquiries," began Holmes, "show that the family portrait did not lie. Stapleton was indeed a Baskerville, son of Rodger Baskerville, Sir Charles's youngest brother who had fled to South America, where he was said to have died unmarried. He did in fact marry, and had one child, his namesake, who married Beryl Garcia of Costa Rica. The younger Rodger, having purloined public money, changed his name to Vandeleur, and fled with his wife to England, where he established a school in Yorkshire. They had met an ailing tutor on the voyage home, and Vandeleur used his ability to make the school a success. But the tutor died, and the school sank finally into infamy. The Vandeleurs changed their name to Stapleton and came to Devonshire.

"Stapleton had evidently made inquiries and found that only two lives stood between him and a valuable estate. To obtain the estate he was ready to use any tool, including his wife, and run any risk. His first act was to establish himself near his ancestral home; his second, to cultivate a friendship with Sir Charles and the neighbors.

"Sir Charles told him about the family hound, and so prepared the way for his own death. Stapleton had learned from Dr. Mortimer that the old man's heart was weak and that a shock would kill him. He had also heard that Sir Charles was superstitious and had taken the legend seriously. Stapleton's ingenious mind suggested the means by which Sir Charles could be done to death. He bought the hound in London, and walked a great distance over the moor to bring it home unobserved. From his insect hunts he had learned to penetrate the Grimpen Mire; there he kennelled the hound and waited his chance. In an emergency he could keep it in the outhouse at Merripit House.

"The problem was to decoy Sir Charles outside at night. Several times Stapleton lurked about with his hound, but to no avail. It was at these times that the peasants saw the hound. He wanted his wife to lure the old man to his death, but she refused; threats and blows would not move her. Then Sir Charles made him minister of some of his charities, and he met Mrs. Lyons. Representing himself as a single man, Stapleton promised marriage in the event of her divorce. Sir Charles's plans to go to London brought matters to a head. Stapleton pressured Mrs. Lyons to send the letter asking for an interview, and on the fatal night prevented her from going.

"He got back to his hound in time to treat it with his infernal paint and bring it round to the alley gate where Sir Charles was waiting. The hound sprang over the gate, and pursued Sir Charles, but it kept on the grassy border so that it left no track. On seeing Sir Charles lying still, the creature probably circled round—it was then he made footprints, some of which were seen by Dr. Mortimer. Both the women in the case, Mrs. Stapleton and Mrs. Lyons, were left with strong suspicions against Stapleton. But both were under his influence; he had nothing to fear from them.

"Learning of Sir Henry's impending arrival, Stapleton's first idea was to kill him in London. He distrusted his wife, who would not help him lay the trap for Sir Charles, but he could not leave her out of his sight lest he lose his influence over her. He took her with him to London, and kept her imprisoned in their hotel room. His wife surmised his plans, but dared not write to warn Sir Henry; she adopted the expedient of sending him the printed-word message.

"It was essential for Stapleton to get an article of Sir Henry's attire, in case he had to use the hound. He must have bribed the hotel boots or chambermaid to help him. The first boot procured was a new one, useless for his purpose. He had it returned, and got an old one—proving to me that we were dealing with a real hound.

"I am inclined to think that Stapleton did not limit himself to the Baskerville affair. During the past few years there have been several vicious unsolved robberies in the west country, and I believe Stapleton recruited his resources in this way.

"Stapleton shadowed Dr. Mortimer and Sir Henry in his cab when they came to Baker Street, and got away from us successfully, sending back his audacious message with the cabman. He knew then that I had taken over the case in London, and that there was no chance for him there. He returned with his wife to Dartmoor."

"One moment," said Watson. "What became of the hound when its master was in London?"

"Stapleton must have had a confidant. I traced the old manservant's connection with the Stapletons as far back as the school days, so that he must have been aware that they were man and wife. It is most probable that he cared for the hound, though he may never have known the purpose for which it was used.

"A word as to how I stood myself at the time you and Sir Henry went down to Baskerville Hall. You may remember that when I examined the paper on which the words were pasted, I made a close inspection for the watermark. Holding the paper a few inches from my eyes, I was conscious of a faint smell of white jessamine. I have made a study of perfumes; the scent suggested the presence of a lady. My thoughts began to turn to the Stapletons.

"It was my game to watch Stapleton. This I could not do if I were with you, since he would be keenly on his guard. I deceived everybody, and came down secretly when I was supposed to be in London. I stayed for the most part in Coombe Tracey, and only used the moor hut when it was necessary to be near the scene of action. Cartwright came down with me, disguised as a country boy. When I was watching Stapleton, Cartwright was often watching you.

"Your reports were forwarded instantly from Baker Street to Coombe Tracey. They were of great service to me, especially the one truthful piece of Stapleton's biography, which helped me to establish his identity. You also cleared up the relationship between the Barrymores and the convict.

"By the time you discovered me on the moor, I had a complete knowledge of the business, but no case for a jury. There was no alternative but to catch Stapleton red-handed. To do so we had to use Sir Henry. At the cost of a severe shock to our client, we completed our case, driving Stapleton to destruction. Sir Henry's love for the lady was deep and sincere; to him the saddest part of this black affair was that he should have been deceived by her.

"It remains to indicate the part Mrs. Stapleton played. Her husband exercised a strong influence over her, through love or fear, or both. At his command she posed as his sister, but she would not be a direct accessory to murder. Paradoxically, he was furious when he saw Sir Henry paying court, although it was part of his own plan. Encouraging the intimacy, he made sure that Sir Henry would be a frequent visitor, giving him, sooner or later, the opportunity he wanted. On the day of the crisis, his wife turned suddenly against him. She knew of the convict's death, she knew that the hound was in the outhouse and that Sir Henry was coming to dinner. She taxed her husband with his intended crime, and a furious scene followed. He told her for the first time that she had a rival in his love. Her fidelity turned instantly to bitter hatred. To keep her from betraying him, he tied her up, and hoped, no doubt, that when Sir Henry's death was put down to the family curse, he could win his wife back to accept an accomplished fact and to keep silent. But I believe that, had we not been there, his doom would have been sealed by his wife. And that, Watson, is the Baskerville story."

"But Stapleton could not have hoped to frighten Sir Henry to death as he had done with Sir Charles," said Watson.

"The beast was savage and half-starved. If it did not frighten its victim to death, it would help paralyze any resistance."

"If Stapleton came into the succession, how could he explain that he, the heir, had been living unannounced under another name so close to the property?" asked Watson.

"Mrs. Stapleton said he had referred to three possible courses. He might make his claim from South America, establish his identity there, and obtain the fortune without ever coming to England. Or he might adopt an elaborate disguise during the time he need be in London, or, again, he might furnish an accomplice with proofs, putting him in as heir, and retaining a claim on his income. No doubt he would have found some way out of the difficulty. And now, my dear Watson, we have a box for the opera, and time for dinner."

Solutions & Epilogues

Puzzle I: *The Boscombe Valley Mystery*

```
S H A D ░ B A H ░ ░ R O S E ░
P A T A ░ O M A R ░ E V I T A
A T O M ░ A I D E ░ W A S A T
R E P A I R ░ F O O L I S H
░ S O D A ░ S A U R ░ ░
W E A K L I N G ░ S N O O P S
H A L ░ E N D E D ░ D O W E L
I S I T ░ G O N E R ░ M E T A
L E C O N ░ R E L E T ░ S A T
E L E M I S ░ S E C R E T L Y
░ A G U E ░ S E A T ░ ░
A N O T H E R ░ S C H O O L
D E F O E ░ S A W S ░ E R N E
J A M E S ░ E L E E ░ R A T S
░ P E S T ░ A D S ░ S L O T
```

"Some two years ago," said Holmes, "when James was only sixteen, and before he really knew Alice, for she had been away five years at boarding school, what does the idiot do but get into the clutches of a barmaid in Bristol and marry her at a registry office? No one knows a word of the matter, but you can imagine how maddening it must have been to be upbraided for not proposing when he would given his very eyes to do so. On the other hand, he had no means of supporting himself, and his father, who was a very hard man, would have thrown him out had he known the truth. It was with this barmaid wife that he spent the last three days in Bristol. Good has come out of evil, however, for the barmaid, finding from the papers that he is in serious trouble, has thrown him over and has written him to say that she has a husband already in the Bermuda Dockyard. I think that bit of news has consoled young McCarthy for all that he has suffered."

At the Assizes, James McCarthy was acquitted on the strength of the number of objections submitted by Holmes to the defending counsel. Old Turner died seven months later, leaving the way open for the son and daughter to live happily together in ignorance of the black cloud which rests on their past.

Puzzle II: *The Five Orange Pips*

E	G	G	S	■	O	F	T	H	E	■	W	A	S	P
R	O	U	T	■	R	E	M	I	X	■	A	N	C	E
A	G	R	A	■	D	R	A	M	A	■	S	T	A	R
S	O	U	T	H	E	R	N	■	M	A	T	E	R	■
■	E	E	R	Y	■	R	I	C	H	■				
C	A	U	S	E	S	■	C	O	N	T	E	S	T	S
O	F	N	O	D	■	T	A	P	E	S	■	T	A	I
N	A	I	F	■	E	B	B	E	D	■	C	E	N	T
E	C	O	■	B	L	O	O	D	■	P	L	A	T	E
S	E	N	T	I	E	N	T	■	R	E	E	L	E	D
■	R	A	C	E	■	M	I	C	A	■				
■	P	L	A	S	T	■	N	I	C	K	N	A	M	E
T	R	O	D	■	O	F	O	N	E	■	E	V	I	L
H	O	N	E	■	R	I	V	E	R	■	S	E	L	L
E	W	E	R	■	S	E	A	R	S	■	T	R	E	S

"I think the State is Texas," said Watson. "What then?"

"I searched the Dundee records, and when I found that the *Lone Star* was there in January, '85, my suspicion became a certainty. I then inquired as to the vessels which lay at present in the port of London; the *Lone Star* had arrived here last week. She left this morning, bound for Savannah."

"What will you do now?" asked Watson.

"Oh, I have my hand upon him," said Holmes. "I learned that Captain Calhoun and the two mates are the only native-born Americans on the ship. I know, also, that they were all three away from the ship last night. I had it from the stevedore who has been loading the cargo. By the time their sailing ship reaches Savannah the mail boat will have carried these pips there, and my cable will have informed the police of Savannah that these three gentlemen are badly wanted here upon the charge of murder."

But the murderers of John Openshaw were never to receive the orange pips. The equinoctial gales were very severe in the year of 1887. The only news about *Lone Star* to reach Holmes was that far out in the Atlantic a shattered sternpost of the boat was seen in the trough of a wave, with the letters "L. S." carved upon it.

P	A	H	S		A	H	M	E		H	E	R	E	S
E	T	O	N		N	E	I	N		E	L	U	D	E
A	T	T	E	N	D	A	N	T		W	E	B	E	R
T	H	E	L	E	A	D			P	A	P	E	R	S
Y	E	L	L	S			H	A	R	S	H			
		S	T	R	E	A	M	S		A	J	O	T	
P	A	T		S	A	L	M	I		N	O	N	E	
O	T	I	C		J	A	M	E	S		T	H	E	M
M	I	L	O			T	E	N	E	R		N	A	P
E	T	T	U		J	E	R	S	E	Y	S			
		N	E	E	D	S		D	E	C	O	R		
W	E	N	T	A	T			T	H	E	T	O	N	E
I	V	I	E	S		O	T	H	E	R	T	H	A	N
S	E	N	S	E		A	R	I	L		L	A	N	D
P	R	E	S	S		R	A	N	D		E	N	D	S

"I have all the proofs I need, but let's make the case complete," said Holmes to Ryder, who had turned pale as a ghost.

"Catherine Cusack told me of the stone," said Ryder.

"I see—her ladyship's maid. You knew this man Horner had been concerned in a robbery before, so the two of you—"

Ryder suddenly threw himself at Holmes's feet. "Have mercy!" he cried. "I never went wrong before! I never will again!"

"Tell the truth, then; there lies your only hope."

"I wanted to hide the stone," said Ryder, "and get it to my friend Maudsley, who had served time; he could turn it into money. My sister, Mrs. Oakshott, had promised me a goose for Christmas. I went to her yard, picked out a white goose with a barred tail, and had gotten the stone down its gullet, when it broke loose and joined the flock. I asked my sister for just that bird. When I got to Maudsley, we found the crop empty. I rushed back to my sister, but she had sold the flock, which had another such bird, to Breckenridge. He would not tell where he had sold it."

Holmes sent the weeping man away. "After all, Watson," he said, "Horner is not in danger; Ryder and Miss Cusack will not appear against him. Besides, it is the season for forgiveness."

Puzzle IV: *The Adventure of the Copper Beeches*

M	R	S	■	C	L	E	A	R	■	W	H	E	N
A	I	L	S	H	O	R	S	E	■	H	A	V	E
I	S	A	T	■	I	D	E	A	S	■	A	L	I	E
D	E	G	R	A	D	E	■	■	T	O	L	L	E	R
■	O	N	E	S	■	C	A	S	E	■			
B	R	I	B	E	D	■	F	O	R	T	■	D	R	S
R	E	S	E	T	■	O	R	A	T	E	■	R	I	P
E	A	R	S	■	T	R	E	S	S	■	T	U	N	E
A	D	E	■	F	I	L	E	T	■	T	E	N	S	E
K	Y	D	■	A	M	O	S	■	L	I	N	K	E	D
■	W	R	E	N	■	G	A	T	A	■			
T	O	K	E	E	P	■	E	D	I	B	L	E	S
E	K	E	S	■	A	R	C	E	D	■	L	A	M	E
A	I	N	T	■	S	O	U	S	E	■	E	D	I	T
M	E	T	S	■	T	O	T	E	R	■	E	L	S

"It was fortunate for Miss Alice," said Holmes to Mrs. Toller, "that Mr. Fowler, being a persevering man, succeeded in convincing you by certain arguments, metallic or otherwise, that your interests were the same as his."

"Mr. Fowler was a very kind-spoken, freehanded gentleman," said Mrs. Toller serenely. "If there's police-court business over all that has happened here, you'll remember that I was Miss Alice's friend."

"Thank you, Mrs. Toller, for clearing up things which had puzzled us," said Holmes. "Here come the country surgeon and Mrs. Rucastle, so I think, Watson, we had best escort Miss Hunter back to Winchester."

Mr. Rucastle survived, but was always a broken man, kept alive through the care of his devoted wife. The Tollers, being privy to certain secrets, still live with them. Mr. Fowler and Miss Rucastle were married by special license the day after their flight, and he now holds a government position in Mauritius. Watson was rather disappointed that Holmes showed no further interest in Miss Hunter once the mystery was solved. She is now the successful head of a private school.

A	N	T	S		S	C	A	R	F			H	I	M
L	O	O	M		A	D	L	A	I		M	E	M	O
P	A	R	I		T	R	A	N	S	P	I	R	E	S
	H	O	L	M	E	S		T	H	E	T	O	T	S
		E	O	S		S	H	Y	E	R				
L	O	A	D	S		A	W	E		L	A	B	E	L
O	F	F			F	R	A		F	E	L	L	T	O
O	T	T		R	A	T	T	L	E	D		A	A	R
T	H	E	B	A	N		T	O	W		C	P	A	
S	E	R	A	C		T	E	T		W	A	K	E	N
			C	H	A	I	R		T	O	R			
M	E	E	K	E	S	T		S	E	W	I	N	G	
A	N	D	A	L	I	T	T	L	E		S	A	I	D
S	T	E	T		G	L	E	A	N		T	I	R	E
K	E	N			H	E	A	V	Y		A	L	L	Y

"What can be the meaning of this?" cried Grant Munro.

"I will tell you," said Effie, sweeping into the room with a proud, set face. "My husband died in Atlanta, my child survived." She opened a silver locket; in it was the portrait of a handsome black man. "John Hebron was my husband—a nobler man never walked on earth. Little Lucy is my own dear daughter."

The child ran to her mother, and nestled against her.

"When I left her in America, it was only because of her weak health. God forgive me, but when I learned to love you, Jack, I feared to tell you about my child. I have heard often from the faithful woman who has been her nurse over the years. At last I had an overwhelming desire to see my little girl. I sent the nurse the hundred pounds, and instructed her about the cottage. I had her cover up Lucy's hands and face, so that if she were seen accidentally at the window, neighbors would not gossip. When you told me the cottage was occupied, I could not sleep for excitement, and so I slipped out. Now you know the truth."

Grant Munro was silent for some moments. Then he lifted the little girl, kissed her, and held out his other hand to his wife.

"We can talk more comfortably at home," he said.

Puzzle VI: *The "Gloria Scott"*—Part 1

O	L	D	A	S	■	C	A	L	I	■	B	A	T	S
F	I	R	S	T	■	O	X	E	N	■	A	N	O	N
O	M	A	H	A	■	M	E	S	S	A	G	E	T	O
R	A	T	A	T	A	T	■	S	I	G	■	N	A	W
■	■	R	E	S	E	W	■	D	E	A	D	L	Y	
■	E	V	E	R	Y	■	I	T	E	R	S	■		
O	P	E	■	S	E	E	T	H	■	S	H	O	W	S
L	E	A	K	■	T	A	H	O	E	■	E	N	O	L
D	E	L	I	A	■	S	T	U	N	G	■	C	R	Y
■	■	E	D	I	T	H	■	D	A	T	E	D	■	
T	R	E	V	O	R	■	E	L	E	V	E			
A	H	A	■	R	E	D	■	A	R	E	T	R	U	E
B	E	G	I	N	N	I	N	G	■	T	H	I	R	D
L	A	R	D	■	I	D	E	O	■	H	E	D	G	E
E	S	E	S	■	C	O	G	S	■	E	R	I	E	S

"I read the message to Victor Trevor. 'The game is up. Hudson has told all. Fly for your life.'

"He sank his face into his shaking hands. 'It must be that, I suppose,' said he. 'This is worse than death, for it means disgrace as well. But what is the meaning of these "head-keepers" and "hen-pheasants"?'

" 'It means nothing to the message. To fulfill the prearranged cipher, the sender would naturally use the first words that came to his mind, and if there were so many that referred to sport among them, you may be sure that he was either an ardent shot or interested in breeding. Do you know anything of this Beddoes?'

" 'I remember that my poor father used to have an invitation from him to shoot over his preserves every autumn.'

" 'Then it is undoubtedly from him that the note came,' said I. 'It only remains for us to find out what this secret was which the sailor Hudson seems to have held over the heads of these two wealthy and respected men.' "

	B	E	E	F	S			W		O	R	T	H	S	
T	E	M	P	L	E		R	A	N	T	R	U	E		
R	A	P	I	E	R		A	L	L	S	I	D	E	S	
E	T	H		D	R	O	S	K	Y			S	I	T	
	S	A	P		A	P	I	E		E	B	O	N	Y	
A	T	T	U			I	N	R	E	V	E	N	G	E	
T	H	I	N	K	I	N	G		R	A	D				
T	E	C		A	C	E		D	I	N		D	I	I	
		A	L	E		S	U	N	S	T	A	N	D		
D	E	S	P	E	R	A	T	E			I	N	F	O	
O	P	A	H	S		M	O	T	H		O	V	O		
E	A	T			A	B	R	O	A	D		I	R	S	
S	C	R	A	M	B	L	E		R	E	A	L	M	E	
	T	A	N	G	I	E	R		K	I	L	L	E	D	
	S	P	A	R	E	D			S	L	Y	E	R		

"And what theory do the police hold?" asked Watson.

"One that is quite the opposite to mine," said Holmes. "They believe that Hudson did away with Beddoes, and fled, but they do not say where. The transport ship *Gloria Scott* was set down by the Admiralty as being lost at sea.

"You have heard the narrative which I read that night to young Trevor, and I think, Watson, that under the circumstances it was a dramatic one. The good fellow was heartbroken about it, and went out to the Terai tea planting, where I hear that he is doing well.

"These are the facts, Doctor, of the very first case in which I used my system, and if they are of any use to your collection, I am sure that they are very heartily at your service."

Puzzle VIII: *The Musgrave Ritual*

C	R	O	W	N	■	R	A	J	A	■	F	O	A	L
L	I	M	B	O	■	O	R	A	N	■	O	R	N	E
A	G	E	N	T	■	C	O	N	C	O	R	D	E	S
N	O	G	■	H	I	K	E	■	I	N	G	O	T	S
G	R	A	V	I	T	Y	■	M	E	D	E	■	■	■
■	■	A	N	I	■	K	I	N	E	T	I	C	■	■
R	E	N	I	G	S	■	I	N	T	S	■	T	O	G
A	L	A	N	■	T	N	G	■	■	S	E	R	E	■
G	I	G	■	S	T	A	G	■	S	T	U	A	R	T
■	A	S	S	O	R	T	S	■	P	H	I	■	■	■
■	■	O	B	I	S	■	D	E	A	T	H	O	F	■
C	A	T	N	I	P	■	S	A	W	N	■	A	F	L
O	F	E	N	G	L	A	N	D	■	T	O	N	T	O
P	O	L	E	■	E	G	A	D	■	H	U	G	H	S
T	R	E	T	■	D	O	P	Y	■	E	S	S	E	S

" 'The crown of the Stuart kings!' cried Musgrave.

" 'Precisely. Consider what the Musgrave Ritual says. "Whose was it?" "His who is gone." That was after the execution of Charles the First. "Who shall have it?" "He who will come." That was Charles the Second, whose advent was already foreseen.'

" 'And how came it in the lake?'

" 'Ah, that is a question that will take some time to answer.' And with that I sketched out to him the chain of surmise and proof which I had constructed.

" 'And how was it that Charles did not get back the crown?'

" 'That is the one point we shall probably never be able to clear up. It is likely that the Musgrave who held the secret died in the interval, and by some oversight left his descendants this guide—the Musgrave Ritual—without explaining the meaning of it. At last it came within reach of a man who tore its secret out of it and lost his life in the venture.'

"That is the story, Watson. Musgrave had some legal bother and a considerable sum to pay to retain the crown. Of Rachel Howells nothing was ever heard. Probably she carried herself and the memory of her crime to some land beyond the seas."

Puzzle IX: *The Adventure of the Solitary Cyclist*

B	E	A	R	D		A	C	E	S		R	U	T	H
A	T	T	A	R		H	A	R	P		E	T	U	I
R	A	M	I	E		E	R	S	E		V	A	N	S
B	L	O	S	S	O	M		C	R	O	S	S		
		E	S	A	S		B	I	O	L				
T	R	A	D	E	S		C	L	E	A	V	E	R	S
H	U	N		R	E	T	R	O		R	E	D	A	N
A	N	A	T		S	H	E	A	F		R	E	N	O
N	I	C	H	T		A	S	T	A	R		M	O	W
E	N	T	R	A	N	T	S		L	E	M	A	N	S
		E	N	E	S		A	S	E	A				
	H	A	W	K	S		B	E	N	N	E	T	T	
B	O	L	O		T	R	I	O		T	E	R	R	A
O	L	A	F		L	O	A	D		E	G	G	O	N
B	E	E	F		E	M	M	Y		R	E	S	T	S

"And she's not your wife, she's your widow!" Carruthers cried. With that, his revolver cracked, and Woodley fell on his back. Williamson pulled out his revolver, but Holmes was too quick for him.

"Drop that pistol!" Holmes cried, his own at the ready. "You, Carruthers, give me your revolver. My name is Sherlock Holmes, and I will represent the police until they arrive." A servant who had appeared on the scene was sent off with a note to the police.

Woodley was carried into the house, and examined by Watson, who said he would live. Carruthers was considerably upset by the news.

"Do not worry," said Holmes. "Williamson had no right to solemnize a marriage, and a forced marriage is no marriage, it is a felony. But why did you not tell Miss Violet of her danger?"

"I fell in love with her and feared she would leave. When this cable came, I knew they would make a move, and I tried to protect her." He handed Holmes a cable which read, "The old man is dead."

Then the rest of the story came out. Violet Smith was next of kin to old Ralph, a very rich man who could not read or write and had made no will. Carruthers and Woodley had planned that one of them would marry her, and share with the other on Smith's death. After they quarreled, Woodley had joined forces with Williamson.

The villains got their just deserts; the groom Peter recovered.

A	L	O	G		S	O	F	A	S		B	L	A	B
N	O	N	A		W	H	I	C	H		E	A	V	E
D	O	L	L		I	N	T	E	R	L	A	C	E	S
	M	Y	L	I	F	E		T	E	E	T	E	R	S
		O	R	T		M	I	D	A	S				
S	W	I	P	E		T	I	C		S	I	N	E	W
H	I	T	S		M	E	S		R	E	T	I	N	A
A	S	I		C	A	N	T	E	R	S		V	A	L
R	E	S	O	L	D		A	Y	S		D	E	C	K
D	R	A	P	E		I	K	E		B	E	N	T	S
		E	V	A	D	E		C	O	D				
C	H	I	N	E	S	E		S	H	O	U	T	S	
R	E	M	A	R	K	A	B	L	E		C	H	I	C
A	M	A	N		E	T	T	A	S		T	A	R	O
B	A	N	D		R	E	U	P	S		S	T	E	W

"It was no brain of a country publican that thought out such a blind," said Holmes. "But let us see what we can see."

There were two unkempt horses in the stable. Raising the hind leg of one of them, Holmes laughed aloud, and said, "Old shoes, but newly shod—old shoes, but new nails. Let us go to the smithy."

A lad working in the smithy disregarded them as Holmes eyed the litter of iron and wood, but the landlord, stepping in behind them, his features contorted with rage, cried out, "You infernal spies! What are you doing here?"

"Why, Mr. Hayes," said Holmes coolly, "one might think that you were afraid of our finding something out."

Hayes mastered himself with great effort, and smiled.

"You're welcome to anything you can find," he said. "You asked me for a bicycle, but I have none. You may have my horses, and the sooner you get out, the better."

"I think we shall walk, after all," said Holmes, and he and Watson walked down the road until the curve hid them from view.

"I can't possibly leave this place, Watson," said Holmes. "We were warm, as the children say. I think we shall now have another look at the Fighting Cock in an unobtrusive way."

A	R	T			W	R	A	P			A	G	N	I
M	E	E	T		R	A	P	I	D		S	O	O	T
B	I	N	E		I	N	O	N	U		K	A	T	E
I	N	S	E	R	T	E	D		C	H	I	L	E	S
	S	E	T	T	E	E		S	H	I	N			
		H	E	R		P	L	E	D	G	E	R	S	
D	U	K	E	S		C	A	U	S	E		C	O	O
T	H	U	S		S	O	L	E	S		S	H	O	P
H	U	R		J	A	M	E	S		W	O	O	D	S
S	H	A	L	I	M	A	R		S	O	N			
		A	B	U	S		O	P	E	N	E	D		
L	E	T	T	E	R		A	R	I	S	E	T	H	A
A	D	I	T		A	U	S	T	L		T	H	O	U
N	A	M	E		I	N	T	H	E		S	I	L	K
A	M	E	R		D	I	E	S			C	E	S	

"James confessed," said the Duke, "that he bicycled to the woods, and told Arthur that his mother was awaiting him on the moor, and that later a man with a horse would take him to her. Poor Arthur fell into the trap. Hayes took Arthur up on his horse, and they rode off together. They were pursued by Heidegger, whom Hayes struck with his stick. Hayes brought Arthur to his inn, where he was confined in an upper room, in the care of Mrs. Hayes, a kindly woman, but under her husband's control.

"James intended to make a bargain with me—if I would break the entail, so that he could inherit my estate, he would restore Arthur to me. What brought the scheme to wreck was your discovery of Heidegger's body. But James pleaded that I give Hayes a chance to save his life. It is settled, Mr. Holmes, that James shall leave me forever and seek his fortune in Australia. And I wrote to the Duchess this morning."

"I am not in an official position," said Holmes, "and so long as justice is served, I need not disclose all that I know. As to Hayes, the gallows awaits him. But I am curious about one thing—where did Hayes get horseshoes that counterfeited cow tracks?"

The Duke led Holmes and Watson to a glass case. Inside were medieval horseshoes that were used to throw pursuers off the track.

H	A	S	P	S		C	U	L			O	D	O	R
O	N	T	A	P		A	R	O	O		R	I	F	E
E	N	U	R	E		P	I	C	T	U	R	E	O	F
D	E	B	A	C	L	E		I	H	N		T	U	I
		D	I	E	T	S		E	F	F	O	R	T	
	B	L	E	A	T		P	E	R	I	L			
B	O	A		L	I	M	A	S		T	A	B	O	R
C	O	D	A		N	O	R	M	A		N	O	N	E
D	R	Y	U	P		T	R	E	N	T		N	E	V
		R	O	M	E	O		I	H	E	A	R		
I	T	W	A	S	A		W	O	M	A	N			
N	R	A		I	L	A		B	A	N	T	A	M	S
C	O	N	S	T	A	B	L	E		T	A	L	O	N
U	P	D	O		R	I	A	S		H	I	L	D	A
R	E	A	D		T	H	E		E	L	I	A	S	

"You compromise me by coming here!" cried Lady Hilda, when Holmes and Watson were shown into her morning room.

"I must ask you, madam, for the missing document. I know of your ingenious entry into Lucas's home last night, of the hiding place under the rug, of the dispatch-box key you have duplicated."

The lady paled. She took the blue envelope from her desk.

"Quick!" said Holmes. "The dispatch box and duplicate key!"

Holmes thrust the envelope among the papers in the box.

"Return the box to your bedroom—and then, the whole truth!"

Lady Hilda had written an indiscreet letter before she had met her husband. "It fell into Lucas's hands. He would give it to me only in exchange for the document—he had learned of it from a spy. We had just made the exchange in his house—the night he was killed—when we heard footsteps. He quickly moved the rug, put the document in its hiding place, and replaced the rug. A woman ran in, screaming in French. I fled. To protect my dear husband, I stole the document back, but did not know what to do with it."

Trelawney Hope and the Premier arrived. At Holmes's urging the skeptical Hope reexamined the box, happily to find the envelope. Privately, the Premier asked Holmes, "How did you do it?"

"We also have our diplomatic secrets," said Sherlock Holmes.

Solutions to
The Hound of the
Baskervilles

Puzzle XIII: *The Curse of the Baskervilles*

C	O	M	B	▪	S	W	I	F	T	▪	T	H	E	▪
A	B	O	U	▪	H	A	N	O	I	▪	H	U	L	L
N	O	R	T	H	E	R	N	E	R	▪	E	G	I	S
T	E	E	▪	O	A	T	S	▪	E	R	N	E	S	T
▪	▪	J	U	R	Y	▪	A	L	E	C	▪	▪	▪	▪
W	O	M	A	N	S	▪	M	E	M	E	N	T	O	
O	N	E	N	D	▪	B	R	A	S	S	▪	E	A	R
D	I	R	E	▪	D	E	A	N	S	▪	N	A	N	A
A	C	C	▪	T	R	A	Y	S	▪	S	E	T	I	N
N	E	I	T	H	E	R	▪	O	H	W	H	A	T	▪
▪	▪	R	E	A	S	▪	I	N	I	T	▪	▪	▪	▪
O	S	T	E	N	D	▪	T	S	A	R	▪	I	O	U
F	I	R	M	▪	F	O	O	T	P	R	I	N	T	S
A	G	I	O	▪	U	V	U	L	A	▪	A	L	O	E
▪	N	O	R	▪	L	A	T	E	R	▪	L	Y	E	S

Puzzle XIV: *The Problem*

S	T	R	A	I	T	▪	▪	▪	C	H	E	R	I	E
C	H	A	R	L	E	S	▪	W	A	I	T	I	N	G
R	E	V	E	L	R	Y	▪	A	M	M	O	N	I	A
A	T	E	▪	▪	S	M	I	T	E	▪	▪	G	A	D
P	A	L	A	C	E	▪	N	E	R	O	S	▪	▪	▪
▪	▪	▪	S	I	R	▪	C	R	A	N	I	U	M	S
N	I	G	H	T	▪	A	L	I	▪	T	A	B	O	O
O	S	L	O	▪	▪	P	E	N	▪	▪	M	E	O	R
R	E	A	T	A	▪	P	M	G	▪	T	E	R	R	E
M	E	D	I	C	A	R	E	▪	B	O	S	▪	▪	▪
▪	▪	▪	N	I	S	A	N	▪	A	N	E	L	E	D
A	N	I	▪	▪	C	I	T	E	R	▪	▪	U	N	I
S	E	D	A	T	E	S	▪	D	R	E	A	D	E	D
S	A	L	T	I	N	E	▪	S	O	T	H	E	R	N
T	R	Y	A	N	D	▪	▪	▪	W	A	S	N	O	T

Puzzle XV: *Three Broken Threads*

```
    P E P     S A I D     L O C K
A R N O     E S N E     I F H E R
D E T E C T I V E     S T A T E
M A R M O T     O P A L     R O C
I C E     H O N I     H E W A S A
T H E R E     A C R O     O D I N
  Y S E R     M E E R     R E S T
    P E P E     P A P S
S H E R     L O C O     H E P S
H A L O     U F O S     E A R T H
E R A S E S     N E O N     I R A
R D S     C H A D     H O L M E S
P E T A L     G E N T L E M A N
A N I T A     A M A H     N E M O
  S C A T     S N E E     D R Y
```

Puzzle XVI: *The Stapletons of Merripit House*

```
  L A Y     P O S T S     B U S Y
T O B E     R A I S E     E S T E
O L E A     O K R A S     L E N T
W A T S O N     R A P I D S
    T H O S     S M E E
T H E Y O U N G     E N V I E D
R E X     S N A R E     T E R S E
E N I D     S P I N A     D A T E
A R L E S     E N T R E     T E D
D Y E I N G     S E T T L E R S
    G A R S     R I C E
  H A N G I T     S H E H A D
M I M I     M A N E T     W E R E
E L A N     E R O D E     A I M S
T A N G     S E T H S     Y R S
```

Puzzle XVII: *Report of Dr. Watson*

```
S A F E ■ H I S ■ ■ A B E L E
E G O S ■ A M I S ■ G R A I L
C R O C ■ M A L I ■ H O S T S
S O D A ■ S M O G ■ A T T H E
■ ■ ■ P L U S ■ N A S H ■ ■ ■
B A L E E N ■ M A S T E R O F
A M I D E ■ P O L A ■ R A K E
R I G ■ G I V E N ■ G A T
E C H T ■ A P E D ■ S C A P E
R E T O O L E D ■ W H O S I S
■ ■ B R A T ■ C A E N ■ ■ ■
W H E R E ■ T W O S ■ V A S T
A E M I A ■ E A C H ■ I C K Y
W E E N D ■ S L O E ■ C H I P
S L U G S ■ T A R ■ T E T E
```

Puzzle XVIII: *Extract from the Diary of Dr. Watson*

```
D I M ■ D A V I D ■ I C E D
A R A T ■ E D I L E ■ N A V Y
B A R R Y M O R E S ■ T R E K
■ E Y E S O R E ■ I N H E R E
■ ■ M A N E ■ A S I E ■ ■
H O B B Y ■ D O L T S ■ M A N
U T I L E ■ F E E ■ R I V E
S H O E ■ A C T E D ■ E L A S
K E G S ■ M A H ■ B L A S T
S R S ■ D A R E S ■ R A N T S
■ T O L D ■ C O A T ■
H I D I N G ■ C O N V I C T
A D A M ■ A P O T H E O S E S
R I D E ■ M A R I E ■ N D A K
M O O R ■ S M E A R ■ S L Y
```

Puzzle XIX: *The Man on the Tor*

	T	A	I	L			A	L	O	H	A			
	W	H	Y	N	O	T		R	A	C	I	N	E	
S	A	U	N	T	E	R		O	U	T	S	I	D	E
H	T	S		O	S	E		I	D	A		M	E	A
A	S	A	N		S	A	I	D		L	A	I	R	S
D	O	N	E	E		T	O	S	S		I	S	L	E
E	N	D	E	A	V	O	R		H	O	L	M	E	S
			R	A	F		T	O	P					
L	O	V	E	L	Y		B	R	E	E	C	H	E	S
O	N	A	N		A	S	I	A		C	R	I	S	P
A	F	L	A	T		C	O	M	E		I	T	S	A
N	I	L		A	N	U		M	L	S		W	E	N
D	R	E	A	M	E	R		E	V	E	N	I	N	G
	M	Y	D	E	A	R		L	E	G	A	T	E	
	S	O	R	R	Y			S	O	P	H			

Puzzle XX: *Death on the Moor*

M	A	K	E	A		D	E	A	D		T	R	I	M
H	E	N	R	Y		A	B	B	E		H	A	R	E
O	R	A	L	E		D	E	C	A	M	E	T	E	R
S	I	R		A	C	A	N	D	L	E		E	N	G
		C	R	O			E	N	T	R	E	E		
S	O	S	O		M	E	N	O	R	A	H			
E	V	E	N		M	A	N		G	E	N	E	T	
N	E	R	V	E		M	O	I		E	D	E	M	A
T	R	A	I	L		A	M	O		E	X	I	T	
		C	A	S	S	I	N	O		E	T	T	E	
T	A	C	T	I	C			D	A	R				
A	D	O		N	A	T	T	I	E	R		N	O	T
M	U	R	D	E	R	O	U	S		I	W	E	R	E
P	L	A	Y		E	R	R	S		S	A	B	L	E
A	L	L	S		D	E	N	Y		E	S	S	E	N

Puzzle XXI: *Fixing the Nets*

```
P I T S  ■  D E A T H  ■  L E T S
A R I A  ■  E N S U E  ■  I D O L
C O N N E C T I O N  ■  S I N E
A N Y  ■  A R E S  ■  N E T T E D
■  E G E R  ■  H E R E  ■
C H A R L E S  ■  I R O N I C
H O N I E D  ■  H E Y S  ■  D L O
E L E C  ■  W E D  ■  A L E E
F L A  ■  E M I R  ■  W A G E R S
■  A R A R A T  ■  D I V O R C E
■  F O C H  ■  E T O N  ■
P A Y F O R  ■  A N N I  ■  S I R
O L E O  ■  A R G U E D  I N T O
S T A R  ■  M O O D S  ■  T O A D
H A R D  ■  E D G E S  ■  A B L E
```

Puzzle XXII: *The Hound of the Baskervilles*

```
■  W A S  ■  L A V A  ■  A B O A T
P O L L  ■  A D I T  ■  L A B O R
T O B E  ■  P A L L  ■  T H E R E
A S S E T S  ■  L A M I N A T E
■  T H E C A S E  ■  H A D
M A S S E  ■  M I T R E S  ■
I S E  ■  A S S N  ■  E Q U A L S
R I A L T O  ■  S U N K I N
E A S T E R  ■  N O T A  ■  I F I
■  D R E W O N  ■  T E N E T
A V S  ■  S E N A T E S  ■
F O O T S T E P  ■  O S P R E Y
O L L I E  ■  P L O W  ■  R A R E
A G A T E  ■  N U K E  ■  I S I N
M A N O N  ■  O S A R  ■  T H E
```